NEARFALL:

JOE REASBECK

Prequel Book 1

"THE ADVENTURES OF MATT AND MIKE"

■ Standel Publishing

Please check out: *www.nearfallbooks.com* and *www.nearfallmovie.com* for updates on upcoming projects.

And stop by the publisher *www.standel.com* to schedule appearances and find book tour information.

Second printing. Printed in the United States of America

ISBN 0-9647721-8-3

© Copyright 2007 by Joe Reasbeck

Cover Design: Ken Harris Graphic Design

*Dedicated to my late Grandmother
who always wanted to be a writer and to my children—
may you always dream.*

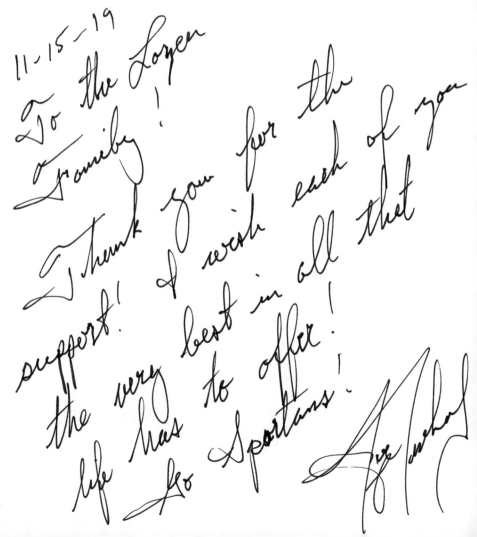

C H A P T E R   1

Matthew Dean stared at the clock. "Ten minutes more until lunch. Ugh, why does the clock move so slow?" His teacher, Mrs. Wilson, was a nice enough lady, but she was yammering on about the making of breakfast burritos. Tomorrow morning, everyone in Matt's fourth grade class was going to be making breakfast for their reading group. "I've made lots of burritos," Matt thought. He shifted from the clock and looked out the windows toward the playground. It had rained last night, and he was looking forward to the lunchtime ritual of "Smear". "Should be a good chance today to get really muddy," he thought. Smear resembled football or rugby, only it was every "man" for himself: translation—everybody against everybody. The last person to the door, carrying the football, was the winner. It was a lot of fun--not that Matt got to play all that often. Smear was reserved primarily for the older kids, the 5th graders, and Matt was usually relegated to the sideline, watching. Not only was he young, but he was also a tad small for his age. His mom had always told him it was because he was sent to school early, due to where his birthday fell on the calendar.

Chapter One

Matt felt someone looking at him. He looked up to see Mrs. Wilson trying to get his attention. "How many times do I have to ask you? What kind of burrito are you planning on making, Matthew?" Apparently, while he was daydreaming and counting the seconds off the clock, Mrs. Wilson had shifted gears. She had started to fill out orders for tomorrow's big feast. "Well?" she inquired. Not knowing the options, Matt just blurted the first thing that came to mind, "El Grande burrito." This got an unexpected roar of laughter from the class. Matt was a bit shocked and a little worried about Mrs. Wilson's reaction, but as the laughs of his "peeps" rolled in, Matt broke out his patented infectious smile. It was his ace in the hole when things got dicey. Mrs. Wilson softened, "All right, that's enough class. Matthew, El Grande is not on the menu. Chicken, beef or cheese?" For a second, Matt thought about asking for combination fajitas, but he could tell by the glint in Mrs. Wilson's eyes that one joke was all that was going to pass. "Chicken please," Matt chirped.

Matt looked over at Kimberly Johnson to see how his comedic timing had affected her. She was smiling at him in what seemed to be a flirty way, or at least that was how he interpreted it. Matt could feel his cheeks get flushed with warmth, and he meekly smiled back. He had never really given girls much thought until this year—well, really until Kimberly. She had pretty green eyes, a few freckles on her nose and long brown hair that she usually wore in a pony tail. To Matt she was the "It" girl. She was a model and movie star rolled into one. Unfortunately, he wasn't the only one who thought so…apparently every boy in 4th grade and more than a few in 5th grade had reached the same conclusion. That, in itself, was amazing, since the older kids never liked the younger ones, not in grade school anyhow or at least his grade school. Undeterred, Matt was convinced that he would marry Kimberly someday…

The bell rang just in time to save Matt from getting too carried away with his wedding vows and mini-van purchase—the mini-van being for their kids, of course. Matt's classmates tumbled out of their desks and spilled out into the hallway. What had seconds earlier been orderly and quiet was now a raucous mass of grammar school humanity. Walking to the lunchroom, Matt spied Kimberly in front of him. He sped up his walk, making his best Nascar sound effects, as he weaved through traffic. When he got within earshot, he pulled it together and tried to act "more his age." He could hear his mother's voice in his head, "Stand up straight, shoulders back. You don't want to be a hunchback, do you?" He made a quick appraisal of his posture and whether or not his shoes were untied. Feeling that everything was in order, Matt pulled up alongside the object of his affection. "Hi," he said, trying to be cool. Kimberly, who had been gabbing with her friend, looked over, gave a quick "Hi" and turned back to her conversation.

Undaunted, Matt tried again, "What are you having for lunch?"

Kim coolly looked back at Matt and replied, "I'm buying my lunch. I'll decide when I see what they have today. What are you having?" Kim looked down at Matt's rolled up paper bag.

Matt was a little embarrassed that he didn't have a cool lunchbox like most of the kids. "I don't know, probably PB&J."

Kimberly actually liked Matt, but there was no way she was going to let him know that. She'd keep him in the game, but she wasn't about to tip her hand. "Well, I was going to say you could stand with me in line if you wanted to, but since you brought your lunch, I guess not." She again turned back to her friend.

Matt was about to give up, but they were rapidly approaching the split. The kids who brought their lunches went to the right and the kids who were buying their lunches went to the left. He knew he had to take his last shot. "What about after lunch? Maybe I could see you outside?" Kimberly looked back at him and smiled broadly. In that instant, all seemed right with the universe. It was the next instant that was the problem. Matt felt a large direct blow to his chest. "Why would she want to talk to a shrimp like you?" Matt staggered back from the push. He looked up into the menacing face of TJ Clark. TJ was a 5th grader and big one at that. In fact, he was usually one of the guys that won the Smear games during recess. Matt gathered himself and tried to stammer out an answer. "I was just..." TJ interrupted, "You were just what?" TJ pushed Matt again, and Kimberly tried to come to Matt's aid. "Leave him alone, TJ." Even though Matt was being humiliated in front of a bunch of kids, he couldn't keep his mouth from smiling ever so slightly at the idea of Kimberly speaking up for him. "What? You sticking up for this little worm?" TJ said mockingly. "I'm not a worm, you big dork." TJ wheeled around. "Uh, oh... me and my big mouth," thought Matt.

"Is there a problem here, Kids?" It was the booming deep voice of Mr. Merrill. Normally, Matt might not welcome the approach of Mr. Merrill, but at this moment, he was very thankful. TJ did his best to cover and make light of the situation. "No, no problem. I was just goofing around with my buddy here." Mr. Merrill turned to Matt, "You OK?" Matt wanted to say no, but with everyone looking, all he could say was "Yes, Sir." Mr. Merrill sized him up to see how much truth there was to that statement. Matt broke out into his signature grin. Mr. Merrill chuckled to himself and then looked at the kids standing in the hallway. "OK, let's get some lunch everybody. The longer you stand out here, the shorter time you have for recess." Everyone shuffled into their respective areas. Matt stood back and let TJ enter the lunchroom first. TJ glared at him, and Matt knew that recess might be a more intense than he had bargained for. After TJ had slipped safely inside, Matt glanced over to see if Kimberly was still looking. She wasn't, but Mr. Merrill was. He bent down and whispered to Matt, "If that guy gives you any trouble, you let me know. Remember I'm bigger than he is." Matt smiled and nodded his head. Mr. Merrill gave him a wink, and continued down the hallway, whistling quietly to himself.

Matt appreciated the sentiment, but he instinctively knew that ratting TJ out to the principal wasn't going to score him any points in the ever-shifting perception of "cool." In order of succession, he'd rather get beat up, tell his brother about it, or tell his parents. Now, if his parents told Mr. Merrill, well hey, that was beyond Matt's control and therefore wouldn't cost him any "street cred" with his classmates. Matt was mulling these options as he took his seat in the lunchroom. TJ was still trying to burn a hole through him with his eyes, and mouthing the words, "You're mine." This threat was a little hard to determine at first because TJ was chewing a mouthful of food, but after the fifth time, it sunk in that Matt still had a problem.

Matt replayed the last few minutes in his head. He felt the whole thing was crazy, and highly unfair. He didn't know that TJ liked Kimberly, and, even if that was the case, TJ didn't own her. Weren't people always saying, "All's fair in love and war?" Matt pondered the slogan. He realized he really didn't understand the meaning previously. He was now starting to understand; certainly TJ seemed to grasp the concept.

Matt reached into his lunch bag and pulled out the contents: two salami and cheese sandwiches, a bag of Cheetos and some grapes. Not a bad haul actually. He looked at the napkin: "Have fun today!" Matt's mom sometimes put little notes in his lunch, and they usually made him smile, but this one just made him roll his eyes. "I wish Mike were here," he thought to himself. Matt's older brother, Mike, was in middle school. He had been in the same school with Matt a couple years earlier, but had now graduated to the next level. "If Mike were here, he'd just do some of those wrestling moves, and this guy would be dust."

5

Chapter One

In truth, Mike wasn't that good a wrestler—at least from the matches Matt had seen. This was only Mike's second season. His first year, he had taken his lumps. However, he was getting the hang of it now, and his results were improving. Most certainly he could handle TJ. Mike was bigger, older, stronger, and knew wrestling. And, as everyone knows, a so-so wrestler is still better to have in your corner then no wrestler at all. But while Matt was having his personal security problems, Mike was having some struggles of his own...

CHAPTER 2

Mike stared at the blank test. He had already thumbed through it a couple times and realized he didn't know anything. Failing this test meant there was a strong possibility that he could fail pre-Algebra, and that would mean he wouldn't be allowed to continue wrestling—definitely not the result he wanted. Mike really liked wrestling. He could feel himself getting stronger, and getting smoother with the technique. It was the toughest sport he'd ever tried, and he enjoyed the challenge.

However, the challenge facing him at the moment was this test, and he didn't like his options. Mike only took pre-Algebra because he was gently forced into it by his father—well that, and there were a couple of really cute girls that were taking the class. Plus, his buddy Dan Morgan had enrolled, and he was always good for a laugh, so it seemed like a good time to get pre-Algebra out of the way.

But as he paged through the test again, it was a lot more conven-ient to blame dear old Dad. "All that talk about the future, getting a good job, math and science being important...blah, blah, blah.

Chapter Two

Why do I need to worry about that stuff now? I'm just a kid. I knew I should have taken wood shop."

He of course knew in his heart, it was his fault. After all, he was the one who hadn't studied. In any case, the "how" and "why" he got into the class didn't change the fact that he was actually in the class and didn't know a thing on this stupid test!

Mr. Rhenkin was sitting behind his desk and would occasionally look up from his newspaper to see if anyone was overtly cheating. He wore a bow tie and a goofy tweed suit with patches on the elbows. For a guy who was probably in his 40s, Mr. Rhenkin looked like someone who had stepped out a time machine and could at any moment break-out into a long discussion about Theodore Roosevelt...not because he was well read, but because he knew the former president personally.

All these random thoughts weren't getting Mike any closer to solving the problems on the test. "Maybe if I just stare at this long enough, I'll remember how to do it." He scribbled a few things down with his pencil and then quickly erased them. After several starts and stops, Mike finally had a breakthrough—he vaguely remembered how to solve one problem, and to his surprise it actually seemed to work. Using the same method, he quickly solved a few more problems. Just when euphoria was about to set in, he ran into a roadblock: the steps didn't seem to work for the next set of questions.

Mike quickly glanced at the clock. He was running out of time. In the next row over, and slightly in front of him, Mike noticed Billy Johnson had already completed his test and was now double checking his answers.

Billy Johnson was the class brain, and was also the subject of ridicule from the rest of the class—not for being a brain, but for being a classic dork. He was soft and pudgy, with jet black hair

NEARFALL:

clipped neatly into a perfect bowl, coke bottle glasses, and more than his fair share of pimples. Billy also had a fascination—many would say an unhealthy fascination—with Greek mythology—gods and goddesses, stuff like that. Not exactly your mainstream, "Hey, did you see that new video on MTV?" type chitchat. Mike had always tried to steer clear of Billy for fear that the "uncool" stigma might leak out of Billy's pores and infect others.

Lately though, Mike found himself talking to Billy. Maybe it was a newfound confidence that was being generated from wrestling, but Mike was starting to care a little less about what other people thought. Besides, some of these Greek dudes seemed pretty cool. Billy even informed Mike that the Greeks were some of the original wrestlers and their gods were known as the Olympians, who sometimes wrestled in battle.

Mike shot a glance in his teacher's direction. Mr. Rhenkin was definitely distracted, seemingly engrossed in his newspaper... probably looking at ads trying to figure out these new fangled modern devices like a car or a dishwasher. Mike decided in that instant, that Billy Johnson was going to be his salvation. He could see Billy's test clearly. Mike put his head in his hand and left some space between his pinky and his ring finger. He looked to see how Billy solved the next batch of questions, "Oh, that's how you do it. I remember that...Why didn't I think of that?"

Mike solved the problems on the second section and then double checked them with Billy's answers. He looked up at the clock—only five minutes left. The third section was all multiple choice or, in Mike's case, multiple guess. He didn't have the slightest idea. It was either answer "B" for all of them, or pray for a miracle. "Come on Billy, turn the page. Check it one more time, you little dough boy."

Two minutes left on the clock. Mike was sweating it. The answers he had would probably get him a "D" but he needed a "C." When all seemed lost, Billy turned the page for one last look. "Yes!" Mike screamed, on the inside. He was copying like mad. Billy looked over his shoulder, caught Mike looking at his answers and quickly leaned forward, blocking Mike's view. With the clock ticking down, Mike was desperate. He strained to see more answers, but Billy had the test shielded from probing eyes.

The bell rang and Mr Rhenkin recited his instructions with all the enthusiasm of a stick. "Time's up, pencils down—bring your tests up front to my desk, and place them face down. Be sure to have your name on them." Billy angrily got up to turn his test in. Mike still had six questions to go. He just randomly filled in A, B, C and D in no particular order and hoped for the best. He turned in the exam, exhaled a sigh of relief, and walked out into the hallway. Dan was waiting for him near the bathroom a few feet down the hall.

"That test sucked," Dan blurted out. "How'd you do?"

The question caused the first twinge of guilt. "I did all right, probably a C, maybe a B." Mike winced; he had never cheated before.

"I bombed it, I'm so screwed. I'm going to get my butt kicked by my father when grades come out." Unfortunately for Dan, when he said he was going to get his butt kicked by his dad, he really meant it. His parents were divorced, and his dad had become a mean drunk. Mike had personally seen Dan get bounced, head first, off a kitchen counter top. His dad just walked behind him, grabbed him at the back of neck, and slammed his forehead into the counter—just for forgetting to take out the trash. Dan was the best wrestler on the team, so it was weird seeing him get thrown around like a rag doll. Dan's mother had remarried and moved out of the state. She had a "new" family now and Dan very rarely saw her.

NEARFALL:

They headed toward their lockers. Mike and Dan had the same homeroom, so their lockers were near each other.

"What are you so quiet for?" Dan asked. It hadn't been five minutes, and already Mike felt like he needed to unburden himself. He felt safe with Dan, they were good buds, and he knew it wouldn't go anywhere.

"I kinda cheated on that test. I copied off Billy."

Dan shrugged, "Yeah, so what?"

Mike tried to explain, "Well, I've just never cheated before, and I'm kinda feeling bad about it."

Dan burst out laughing, "Oh please! Give me a break. You can be such a nerd sometimes. I'd still be in grade school if I didn't cheat."

Mike looked at him with a little skepticism. Sometimes Dan stretched the truth to make himself seem more of a rebel than he actually was. "I didn't know that."

Dan put his books away while Mike fumbled with his lock. "Yeah, well it's not exactly something I advertise. Like today, I was trying to cheat off Vanessa, but she knew it and kept covering up her paper. She's so uptight. But did you see that sweater she was wearing today—oh my…"

Mike responded. "Maybe she just doesn't like you."

Dan quickly dismissed the notion, "Puh, like that's possible, I've got her eating out of my hand."

Michael chuckled at his buddy's misguided bravado. "Yeah, I can see that."

11

Chapter Two

Dan shut his locker. "Hey, I've got to get to gym and work my magic with Pamela."

"Your magic? Mike asked. "Aren't you square dancing today for gym? And besides, don't you have a girlfriend?"

Dan waved him off, "Mike. Mike. Mike, that was so last week. Stay up to speed brother. You know I can't be saddled during square dancing. Yee haw! Actual physical contact with a girl!"

"Well, that ought to be a first for you. Congratulations," Mike replied sarcastically.

Dan was walking down the hall backwards trying to get his last sparring in with Mike. "I've brushed up against more than you have, Pardner!" He stuck his thumbs in his belt loops and started to dosey-do. Unfortunately for Dan, he spun right into Mrs. Harrison, the 8th grade history teacher—a linebacker of a woman. Dan stumbled back from the collision.

"You'd better watch where you're going or someone's going to get hurt," Mrs. Harrison warned.

"Yes Ma'am, I mean Mrs. Harrison. I'm sorry." Mike was laughing nearly to the point of tears.

Although this banter with Dan was lighthearted and fun, the gnawing guilt hadn't completely subsided. As he walked to English, he could hear his dad's voice in his head, "Now I want you to understand that there are certain responsibilities that come with being an older brother. Your younger brother is going to do what you do. And if you are a poor example of behavior, he's going to feel justified in doing those things too. He's going to be watching you, so if you care about your brother, you keep yourself on the straight and narrow. There's going to be peer pressure, but I know you're strong. Just remember, when you hear, 'everybody does it' more often than not, it isn't something you should be doing."

Mike ducked in the door, and shuffled to his desk just as the tardy bell rang. He plopped himself down. He must have heard that little speech from his parents, in one form or another, twenty times the summer before heading into middle school. As Mike settled in, he pulled out the required reading, The Last of the Mohicans. "Well, that's just great, a book about honor and courage." Mike let out a heavy sigh. "I wonder how Matt is doing today?"

Matt had drawn out eating his lunch for as long as he could. There was no one left in the lunchroom except himself and the janitor. "Not good—this is definitely not good. I can't stall anymore."

Matt threw his paper sack with the remains of his lunch into the trash. Not a glamorous last meal for a condemned kid, but it hit the spot. TJ had already gone outside with his buddies, and from all appearances he hadn't had a change of heart. Matt thought about perhaps hiding in the bathroom during recess, but instinctively he knew that would make him the biggest weenie in the entire grade school.

Certainly hiding like a little mouse wasn't going to score any points with Kimberly...but then again neither was getting beat to a pulp. He wondered if this is how it felt for prisoners when they went before the firing squad. A blindfold might be appropriate; it was likely to be an ambush the moment he stepped outside. Only a few feet now separated him from the door leading to the courtyard. Matt could feel his stomach tighten and his legs felt a little rubbery as he reached for the handle. He took a deep breath, steadied himself, and pushed the door open...

CHAPTER 3

Matt pushed open the door half expecting a brick in the face. The mid-day sun was so bright, that coming from the darker cafeteria lunchroom it was nearly blinding. Matt squinted and looked in all directions. He couldn't see TJ. In fact, he couldn't see much of anything.

As his vision adjusted, he came to the conclusion that perhaps he didn't have as much to worry about as he previously thought. TJ was nowhere in sight and neither was the brick or any other heavy blunt object. There was just a mass of kids doing all the normal things at recess. Matt pondered the situation, "Maybe TJ is like one of those dogs that is all bark, no bite. They look vicious, but they're really not."

He relaxed a little, and started to look around for some of his buds—or better yet, Kimberly. Just when he thought the coast was clear, he saw Sarah Conner running up to him. Sarah told everyone to call her Jasmine, which was her middle name. She was tired of everyone doing their Arnold Schwarzenegger impersonation while pretending to kill her.

NEARFALL:

"Sarah Conner?" everyone would say in a big Austrian accent.

"I guess after the one thousandth time you've heard the line, it ceases to be funny." Although he still found it amusing that as she came toward him, what he heard in his head was Arnold's voice, "Sarah Conner?"

In any case, Matt didn't take it as a good sign that the Terminator victim was the one coming to deliver him a message. It was a little like the Ghost of Christmas Future coming to show you your tombstone.

"TJ wants you to meet him by the handball courts," Sarah breathlessly blurted out.

"OK, thanks." Matt shook his head with disbelief. "This guy wants me to voluntarily walk over and make it easy for him? No way, no how...I'm not doing it!" As this thought raced through Matt's brain, he felt the gaze of dozens of kids.

Matt looked around, everyone in his class was looking right at him—including Kimberly. The realization hit him that there seemed to be some sort of expectation, as though he were nominated the fourth grade sacrificial lamb. If Matt were slaughtered, maybe the rest of them would be spared? Or maybe they just wanted someone to stand up to the tyrant? Either way, Matt could see this wasn't going to end by staying away.

As insane as it seemed, Matt turned and started walking toward the handball courts. It was obvious why TJ wanted to meet him there. The teachers' aides who patrolled the playground during recess, usually stayed in the section of the playground where the youngest children were. They would make an occasional stroll through where the older kids were hanging out, but only once during an entire recess would they pass by the handball courts. It was the perfect place…if you wanted to do something you weren't supposed to do.

Matt resigned himself to his fate, and surprisingly the fear subsided a little, "How bad could it really be?" He made up his mind to take it like a man. No matter what, no matter how much it hurt, he wouldn't cry. Matt rounded the corner to the handball courts, and there was TJ with about 15 of his friends. Matt stepped onto the court, and TJ, who had been leaning against the wall, stepped out to greet him. Matt looked around as TJ's goons encircled the two of them.

"So, the little worm showed up. How about that? Hey, the tallest of you guys stand in front of the opening, and try to make it look like you're not standing guard."

The fear that had subsided just moments earlier came rushing back in a surge of adrenaline. Matt could feel his hands shaking.

"OK, Worm, let's get it on!" TJ raised his hands like a boxer.

Matt looked at him with a fair amount of skepticism…The thoughts sped through Matt's brain, "Is he just going to stand there? Does he expect me to walk into his fist?"

Matt blurted out, "Do you even know why you want to beat me up?"

The question seemed to knock TJ off balance, as if it was too much for his primitive brain to comprehend. Seeing this, Matt continued, "You don't, do ya? So what are we doing this for? This meeting is done. I'm outta here."

TJ stood there stunned. However, when Matt tried to get past the goons, they blocked his path. By this time TJ's brain had finally recovered. "Get back here, Worm! We ain't done with nothing!"

The range of emotions that Matt was feeling jumped all over the map. Anger flashed through him. "I'm not a worm, but you're an idiot. Hey, let's play a quick game: I'll take 'morons' for $500. My name starts with the letter T and ends in the letter J and they're not my initials. Give up? What's the capitol of Iowa? How about Minnesota? How do you find your way home from school? Do you know your address? What is - I have no idea!"

Like a bull seeing a red flag waving, TJ finally charged - he had had enough of Matt playing gameshow host.

TJ's first punch missed Matt's face and actually hit him in the shoulder, but even that felt like a mule kick. Matt threw a punch of his own that bounced off TJ's chest. TJ's next punch connected square with Matt's left cheek, snapping his head back. The next hit his mouth and nose and Matt could hear the crunch. His legs crumpled underneath him. More than a little dazed, he fell into TJ. Matt couldn't hold himself up, and blood was pouring from his mouth. TJ held him up with one hand, and continued punching him with the other. Matt bit his tongue on an uppercut, but most of the shots now were to his body. It felt like his ribs were caving in every time TJ connected.

TJ let go, and Matt fell to the ground, barely aware of his surroundings. TJ stood over him, "Stay away from Kimberly, Worm!"

With that announcement, it was over. TJ and his buddies walked off, leaving Matt bleeding and sprawled out face first on the ground. Matt closed his eyes; he could feel the coolness of the concrete on his face. However, that sensation was quickly replaced by the warm wetness of his own blood.

He tried to make an assessment of his condition. Matt moved his

Chapter Three

fingers and his feet—he could breathe OK, so the big functions seemed to be in place. He gingerly pushed himself up to a sitting a position and leaned his back against the wall. He was still a bit woozy. He leaned on his left hand to help steady himself, and with his right hand he touched his face to see if all the pieces were where they were supposed to be. Matt was pleasantly surprised to find that they were.

He had a big welt under his left eye, he could feel that his nose was bleeding, and his lip was split. Matt opened his eyes. They fluttered a bit at first, as if not too sure that he should actually be conscious. Eventually, the world came into focus. Matt spit out some blood and felt something hard in his mouth. He grabbed the nugget, and dropped it into his hand. It was a tooth, or part of a tooth. On closer examination, he was relieved to find that it was only a baby tooth.

Matt stuck the tooth in his pocket just as the bell rang. A sly smile crept across Matt's face. He didn't cry. Not only did he not cry, he might even be able to con the tooth fairy into coughing up some dough. Matt got to his feet like an old man, and started to make his way to the nurse's office. He began rehearsing his speech to explain how he fell face first playing Smear. He knew he could pull the wool over the nurse's eyes and, most likely his parents'. It would be tougher explaining it to his brother. Mike had played Smear; he'd know it was unlikely to have gotten this banged up. "Maybe it wouldn't be such a bad idea telling Mike the truth— he'd go ballistic and beat the snot out of TJ."

As Matt entered the school, he was still dripping blood occasion- ally, the little crimson droplets visible on the polished tile of the school floor. But Matt scarcely noticed. His mind was dominated by one question, "What am I going to tell Mike?"

Mike tried to take his mind off his cheating "scandal" by thinking about other things. As the school day drew to a close, his mind wandered from thought to thought. "Why are all the blackboards in this school actually green? And since they're ALL green why do the teachers still say blackboard? Why not greenboard or chalkboard?"

He wished he'd eaten more for lunch. He was feeling hungry. It would be hours yet before his next meal. Mike wondered what his mom had up her sleeve for dinner. His dad had been out of work for six months, so money was tight, and sometimes Mom had to be pretty creative. No one ever went hungry. It was just an eclectic menu. The previous evening, the fare included a vegetable omelet as the main course, with a side of macaroni and cheese.

Mike was worried about his parents. The tension was mounting. They did their best to hide it, but Mike knew his parents had been fighting. He had heard their raised voices in the bedroom this morning while he ate his breakfast.

Mike's father was a proud man, and it wounded him deeply that he had lost his job. He had worked twenty years for the same company. The last five years he was on the job, he was the union rep and had been doing pretty well. However, when the economy tanked, the company suffered.

As the union rep, he worked with the management on a new contract. He'd seen the books. He knew the company wouldn't survive, if the union didn't take the deal. He did his best to convince them, but of course the union rejected the contract. As predicted, it didn't take long before the company ran out of cash, and everybody lost their job, including Mike's father, Peter Dean.

When it all came down, he remembered his dad saying that it was a lesson about cutting off your nose to spite your face. Mike figured it was like shooting a double leg takedown with your head

19

Chapter Three

down, and your arms stretched out like an eagle. Not only will
you not get the takedown, but there's a real good chance you'll get
thrown to your back.

Dan had agreed to meet Mike immediately after school at the Mill
House, which was a combination gas station and convenience
store. They often would split a box of Toaster Tarts before
wrestling practice. Mike knew he probably shouldn't eat before
working out, but the Toaster Tarts had some vitamins, and, anyway, it had to be better than getting a candy bar. Besides, he and
Dan only ate the unfrosted ones.

Mike's stomach pangs were kicking in big time as the bell
rang. He was out the door in a flash and down the granite steps
in the front of the school. The Mill House was directly across
the street. Mike had it timed so that, if he hustled and was for-
tunate to get a WALK sign at the corner traffic light, he could
be at the Mill House in less than thirty seconds from the time
the bell rang.

Mike looked at his watch as his feet hit the sidewalk in front of
the store. Twenty nine seconds. "Not bad, not bad," Mike thought.
He dug in his pockets to see what kind of funds he was working
with. Mike counted out the change, it totaled eighty nine cents.

While Mike was counting, Dan had snuck up behind him, and
looked over Mike's shoulder. "Guess I'll be sporting for more
than half. That's two days in a row, you bum."

Mike glanced back and saw Dan peeking over his shoulder.
"Yeah, well, you can have three extra crumbs. I'm starving.
Besides, you should just be happy I'm willing to be seen with
you."

They made their way into the store and headed for the aisle with the Toaster Tarts. The bell on the front door started clanging, announcing that someone was coming in. Dan looked back, and elbowed Mike. "Hey, it's Pamela and a couple of friends."

Mike stayed focused on the task at hand. "Yeah, so what?"

Dan looked at Mike like he had lost his mind. "What do you mean, so what? Pamela, you know Pamela, the girl I was working my mojo with during gym?"

Mike looked up from trying to decide whether to go with blueberry or strawberry. "Oh yeah, Pamela. She's cute."

Dan nearly fell over in disbelief. "Cute? Come on, she's better than cute. Are you telling me you are more interested in that Toaster Tart box than going over and chatting with the ladies?"

Mike grabbed the blueberry box. "Yep, that's what I'm telling you. Now give me your money, so we can go eat these."

Dan handed over a buck. "All right, you go pay. I'll catch up with you outside."

Mike hustled to the checkout counter. As the cashier rang up the purchase, Mike glanced back to see Dan clowning with the girls. "If he doesn't make it outside in two minutes, I'm eating his too,"

Mike threw the receipt in the garbage and headed outside. He ripped open the box and the foil bag holding the contents. Mike smiled at the taste of that first bite.

"You eat that thing like you've never seen food before," sneered Lance Olsen. Lance was an arrogant hockey player who thought he was God's gift to everything. They had some of the same friends, but Mike barely tolerated him.

21

Chapter Three

"Yeah? Why don't you shut up Lance, before I stuff you in the dumpster out back."

"Whoa, tough guy," Lance mockingly smiled his cheesy grin as he ducked inside the store.

Mike glared at him just long enough to see him drop out of sight, and then merrily went back to consuming the Toaster Tarts.

After polishing off his half of the pastry bounty, Mike kept looking back at the store to see if Dan was coming. "If he doesn't get out here in one minute, he'll be going hungry." Mike glanced at his watch. They only had a few minutes before they needed to be at practice anyhow.

He peered into the box and started to pull apart the packaging on Dan's half. Just then Dan, Pamela, Lance and the others came piling out of the store. Now that his stomach was a little full and his brain was capable of thinking about other things, Mike noticed that in addition to Pamela, who was very pretty, one of the other girls was Stacey Orlaski, a girl that Mike had a little crush on—although he would never admit it to anyone.

He stood up as the group approached. "Hey, did you save any for me?" Dan asked. Mike nodded as he handed Dan the box; he made eye contact with Stacey and she gave him a little smile. Mike quickly looked away, feeling somewhat embarrassed. Lance spoke up, "Hey, my brother has got some blunt and we're going to my house for a little party - you in?"

Mike wasn't certain he heard the question properly. "Blunt?"

This got a laugh from everyone and Mike felt stupid.

"Yeah blunt, you know, marijuana, geez look at this guy - you sure you didn't start without us? You're already downing the munchies."

"Come with us, Mike. It'll be fun, won't it Stacey?" Pamela gave her friend a sly look and the two girls tittered with laughter.

Stacey looked mischievously at Mike. "Yeah it would be fun."

For a moment Mike hesitated, but then Lance sealed his decision.

"You're not scared are ya? Come on, it's no big thing. Everybody does it."

Mike could feel his jaw tighten. Oh, how he'd like to knock that smug look off of Lance's face. "No, I'm not scared. I've got wrestling practice."

Dan piped up, "We can miss one practice. It's not going to kill us." Dan was looking at Mike with a pleading look that said, "Dude don't screw this up for me, I've got a chance with Pamela."

Mike was shocked and disappointed with Dan, especially to see him standing in the same camp as Lance. "No, we really can't miss practice, Coach will KILL us, Dan."

Mike added emphasis to the word kill to remind Dan that not only would their coach be angry, but it was quite likely that he'd be calling Dan's dad. And that would surely mean a beating for Dan. Not because Dan's father gave two nickels about whether or not Dan actually attended practice. He'd just be angry that someone from the school called him. It didn't matter the reason. Mike looked at Dan squarely. "We're going to be late for practice - let's bounce."

For five seconds, no one said anything, all eyes were on Dan. Five

Chapter Three

seconds seemed like an eternity. Mike could see the conflict in Dan's eyes. Mike said again, "Come on, let's go, we're already going to be doing laps for being late."

Mike started to turn toward the school, when Dan made his decision. "I think I'm going hang with these guys today. Tell Coach I wasn't feeling good." Mike looked at Dan with displeasure, but Dan was already basking in the loving glow of Pamela's attention.

Mike turned and walked by himself toward the school. "This day has really sucked," Mike thought. "I cheated on a test, my parents are probably fighting, my best friend is skipping practice to go do drugs, and the girl I like thinks I'm a geek. What else could possibly go wrong?"

Matthew was sitting in the alley behind the Dean home with his face looking like a badly bruised apple. He was anxiously waiting for Mike to get home from wrestling practice...

CHAPTER 4

Matt's teeth were starting to chatter as he picked at the worn and cracked paint. He had been perched on the top rail of the fence for nearly a full hour, and with the sun setting, it was beginning to get cold. "I wish I would've grabbed a jacket," Matt thought to himself.

He had told his mother that he was taking his bike out for spin around the neighborhood. She had glanced dutifully out the kitchen window as he exited the back gate. Matt was generally a good kid, a bit rambunctious at times, but usually well-mannered. However, with his face looking more lumpy than usual, keeping an eye on him seemed appropriate.

What she couldn't see was that Matt simply walked to the other side of the garage, leaned his bike against the fence as a makeshift ladder, and scampered up. The fence ran alongside the Dean house and made an "L" with the backside of the garage. This section of the fence was obscured by an overgrown lilac bush and some hedges that hadn't been clipped in awhile.

Chapter Four

"Practice must have run late," Matt thought to himself. He gazed down the alley waiting for his brother to turn the corner. As he waited, he mulled over, for what seemed like the hundredth time, how to best present what he wanted to say. He knew there wouldn't be much time for small talk. His punching bag of a face would bring things to a head quickly. Leading off with "So how was practice?" wasn't going to cut it. Matt took a deep breath and exhaled; getting his story past his Mom was relatively easy. Keeping Mike from storming TJ's house…that might be more of a challenge.

Matt tried to distract and amuse himself. He mumbled aloud as he examined the various paint chips he had pulled off, "This fence has been painted four different colors."

A man's voice interrupted Matt's world. "Actually, it's more like five, but who can tell the difference between classic white and antique white?" Matt looked up startled, he hadn't heard his father open the back gate. "What are you doing out here anyhow?"

It took a moment for Matt's brain to engage. "Ahh, I dunno, just bored I guess."

His Dad looked him over. "I understand that you had a little mishap at school? Your mother told me that things got a little rough playing football?"

Matt kept his head down and continued to pick at the fence. "Yep, two big kids landed on top of me, and my face got smashed."

His Dad eyed him skeptically. "Well, it's getting cold and it's almost time for dinner, so why don't you come in and wash up?"

Matt sensed that Pops wasn't really buying the story, so he went to his old reliable. As his father turned to walk back to the house,

NEARFALL:

Matt gave him his trademark grin. "Hey Dad, does the tooth fairy still give out cash for teeth?"

His Dad chuckled. "We'll see, although I think there should be a discount for molars."

"Aww, come on, molars are bigger." Matt pleaded.

Mr. Dean acknowledged Matt's argument. "I'll talk it over with the tooth fairy and your mom. In the meantime, I'll offer you some advice...when playing football in the future; try to break your fall with something other than your face, just a tip. I'll see you inside."

"Ha Ha, you're funny Dad." His dad smiled and disappeared around the side of the garage.

"Whew, another bullet dodged," Matt thought. Matt peered down the alley again. "When is he going to get here?" Sure enough, rounding the corner, there was Mike. Even though it was getting dark there was no mistaking his familiar outline. It would just be moments now. He could feel himself tensing. "I'm more nervous to tell my brother I got my butt kicked than I was about the actual fight."

Mike kicked the rock again, he'd been kicking it for the better part of a block, but as he neared the alley it was difficult to spot amongst the other rocks. He spied his target and lined up for yet another last second field goal. The rock shot out from the side of his foot, ricocheting off several other pebbles before coming to rest in the grass on the side of the alley. Mike quickly made his calculation. The rock, while having provided mind-numbing entertainment for the last several minutes, had now lost its appeal. Trying to dislodge it from the grass seemed like too big an effort. Besides, he had already won so many games with his

Chapter Four

last second 50 yard field goals that enshrinement in the Hall of Fame was a lock. He was tired, cold, and hungry. All he wanted to do was get inside the house, get warm, feed his face, and drop into bed.

As he got closer to the garage, he was surprised to see Matt jumping down from the back fence. "What's he doing?" Mike thought. He took his hand out his pocket and waved. Matt waved back.

"Hey dork? Isn't dinner ready?"

Matt was looking down and took a couple steps toward Mike. As Mike approached, he set off the motion light their father had installed on the garage. Matt knew his face would be in full view. Matt looked up and immediately Mike stopped in his tracks.

"What the heck happened to you? Are you all right?"

"Yeah, I'm all right."

Mike could see from the look in Matt's eyes that these weren't self-inflicted wounds. This wasn't a "hey let's see if we can jump the ditch with our bikes" type of injury. In an instant, Mike could feel the anger inside him go white hot. "Did this happen at school? Who did this to you? Was there more than one? I want names, I want addresses!"

Just as Matt expected, the questions were coming rapid fire and with intensity. And without a doubt, there was a part of Matt that would love to fan the flames and turn his brother loose on TJ, but Matt had decided on another course of action. He'd certainly had plenty of time to think about things from recess to now.

"Mike, hey take a breath. His name is TJ Clark. He's a 5th grader, but I don't want you to touch him."

NEARFALL:

Mike shot Matt a bewildered look. "What are you talking about? I'm your brother. Of course I'm going to pound this guy. Matt, you don't have to worry, when I get done with him, he'll never bother you again."

Matt nodded in agreement, "Yeah I know, I wouldn't be worried about him coming after me again."

Mike was confused. "Then what's the problem?"

Matt shrugged and blurted out, "I want to do it myself! I just want to do it myself." His voiced cracked with emotion—much to Matt's surprise. His eyes filled with tears, and he struggled to blink them back. "I want to learn to wrestle. Will you teach me?"

Mike immediately cooled down. It pained him to see his brother so upset. "Yeah, of course, Buddy. I'll teach ya. How big is this kid?"

Matt looked Mike over. "He's about your size."

"Wow, so he's a big 5th grader."

Matt had recovered some. "Nah, you're just a puny 7th grader."

In truth, Mike was bigger than TJ, but Matt loved to give his older brother a hard time. On most nights this little jab of sarcasm would surely have garnered Matt an "I'll show you puny" charley horse or at the very least a slug in the shoulder. But tonight Mike just smiled.

"So, do you know if this TJ kid wrestles?"

Matt thought for a second. "Nope, he plays hoops."

Mike put his hand on his younger brother's shoulder. "We have a saying in wrestling—our favorite thing on a basketball floor is wrestling mats door to door. In two months you'll be ready for a rematch with this guy."

"Really?" Matt asked in a hopeful voice, "You think I can take him?"

Michael was confident in his answer. "If you work at it, I don't have a doubt in my mind. But you've gotta work at it—I can show you the moves, but it isn't like waving a magic wand. You've gotta practice a lot."

Matt was resolute with his response, "I will, I promise."

Mike stuck out his hand. "Shake on it?"

Matt eagerly grabbed his hand and shook it vigorously. Mike smiled. He was glad to have "solved" the problem, but now it was back to other pending business. "OK. Cool. Let's get something to eat, I'm starving."

Mike and Matt headed toward the house. "By the way, what did you tell Mom and Dad?"

"I told them I got buried face first playing Smear."

"Hey, that's not bad—did they buy it?"

They climbed the back steps, and Matt answered, "Mom did, but I'm not sure about Dad."

"All right, no problem. I'll back ya, if the subject comes up. Why did this kid beat you up anyhow? Let me guess. Your mouth overloaded your butt."

Matt looked at him with disbelief. "No, that wasn't it."

NEARFALL:

"Well, what was it then?"

Fortunately for Matt, it was dark out now because he was blushing. Finally, he sheepishly squeaked out, "It was about a girl."

Mike dramatically clutched his chest as if he was having a heart attack. "WHOA! A girl? A girl? Oh my! Stop the press! Matt's got a girlfriend."

Matt stopped at the back door before going in. "Shh, Shut up, you're going to blow it. She's not my girlfriend. I just kind of like her, and apparently, she's spoken for." Matt gestured to his face as a way of stating the obvious.

Mike just giggled in a hushed voice, "Mattie's got a girlfriend. Mattie's got a girlfriend."

They rolled into the house and Matt muttered, "It's sometimes hard to believe that you're the older brother."

As the Deans sat down to dinner, they surveyed the leftovers from the last several nights. Dad and Mom led them in thanks and, with the prayer done; Mike was finally on the cusp of filling his growling stomach.

The door bell rang just as Mike was in the process of cutting off a big slab of meatloaf. His mouth watered in anticipation as he guided it to his plate. The door bell impatiently rang again. His father spoke up. "Michael, could you get the door please?"

For a moment Mike gave a pleading look as if to say "Why me? Why not someone else?" but he quickly abandoned it. He knew pursuing that any further would just ensure that his list of nightly chores would be lengthened. Mike put down the spatula and plodded off to the door. "Probably UPS or some political campaign," Michael thought as he flung open the door.

Chapter Four

However, standing in front of him was his best friend, Dan, wasted out of his mind.

"Dude, you gotta help me. I can't go home. I'm so messed up." Dan was swaying on the landing. His pupils were dilated, and he stunk of pot and booze.

"Well, you can't stay here. What are you thinking? My parents are here — we're eating dinner."

"Dude, you gotta let me in. They're after me. They're after me, Mike." Dan seemed scared.

"Who's after you?"

Just then his dad called from the dining room, "Mike, who's at the door?"

Mike's mind raced. What was he supposed to do? Dan tried to steady himself with the handrail. He pleaded with Mike, "I need your help, Bro. They're going get me. I can't let my dad see me like this."

Mike's dad's voice grew more impatient. "Michael?"

"Yeah Dad. Be right there." Mike had to move fast. The meatloaf would have to wait....

CHAPTER 5

Mike looked into Dan's glazed and dilated eyes and grabbed him by the arm. "You remember where my room is?" Dan nodded in the affirmative. "All right. Go up and crash. I'll be up after dinner." Mike again looked at his friend, not sure if what he was saying was registering. Mike heard his dad's chair push back from the dinner table. "Go!" Dan's eyes widened as Mike gave him a shove. Dan took off, clumsily running up the stairs, and Mike wheeled around to head back to dinner.

His dad broke stride when he saw Mike entering the room. "What's all the racket? Who just ran upstairs?"

Mike tried to seem as casual as possible. "Oh that was just Dan. We're going to study for a test after dinner." Mike looked at his dad to see if that would end the inquiry. He could tell from the furrowed brow that it would not.

"Well, why didn't he come in and say hello?"

Mike shifted on his feet, his mind desperately grasping for an

Chapter Five

answer; fortunately, his mom piped in, buying him some time. "Would Dan like some dinner? There's plenty here."

The mention of food helped Mike lock into a line of reasoning. "I asked him, Mom, but he said he already ate." Looking back up at his father, Mike continued, his voice lowering in volume to indicate that he was saying something that was best discussed in the company of men. "And that's why he ran upstairs; I guess he's having some gas or something."

Almost on cue, Dan made some sort of inhuman groan from the second floor of the Dean house. Mike winced, wondering if it was too pathetic and might merit further investigation, but his dad chuckled, "I understand."

"Whew! He bought it." Mike felt as though he might have a heart attack as they walked back to the dinner table. "How am I going to get Dan out of the house?"

He took his seat. He could feel Matt looking at him. He glanced up to see Matt shoveling in cornbread and giving him a look like, "Hey, what's going on?" Despite the seriousness of the situation, Mike could feel the corners of his mouth start to curl up in a smile. Matt looked so goofy. His bruised and swollen face had a certain chipmunk quality, making it seem as though he was stuffing the cornbread into storage for an after dinner snack. Mike quickly clamped down his lips and shook his head as if to say, "No, don't go there. I'll tell you later." Matt picked up on it immediately. Unfortunately, so did his mother.

She could sense these two kids of hers were up to something. However, unless she was really mad, it usually wasn't her style to ambush immediately. She was more methodical in shaking the truth out. Like a police officer doing an interrogation, she'd ask the same question, or variations of the same question to see if the accused could keep the facts straight. Usually, if she gave her boys enough rope, they'd hang themselves.

Mike was finally digging into his meatloaf when the first question came. "So, Dan didn't want any dinner?"

Mike swallowed before answering, "No, he already ate."

"Are you sure? Because he usually is a bottomless pit. I've never seen Dan turn away a meal in all the years you've known him."

Mike fidgeted a little in his seat. "Well, he's not feeling so hot. I think he's got an upset stomach."

Mom let it sit for a few seconds as Mike gulped down some more food. "So, what did he have to eat? Do you know?"

This should have been an easy one to handle, but Mike panicked as he grasped for a menu item. The way his mother placed emphasis on the "do you know" portion of the question, it screeched through Mike's brain as, "If you were telling the truth, you'd know what he ate."

His mom continued the investigation. "Well, if you don't know what he had to eat, how do you know that he's sick from something he ate?"

Mike looked across the table to see if Matt could bail him out, but he had his head down and was only focused on chewing. No way was he going down with the ship.

Mike's dad, who had been happily dishing himself a third portion of scalloped potato surprise, seemed unaware that his wife was on the hunt. "The kid just has some bad gas. I'm sure he'll be OK."

35

Chapter Five

Mama Dean narrowed her eyes at her husband, and he shot back a befuddled look as if to say, "What are you mad at me for?" When she softened to a little smile combined with a twinkle in her eye, he knew she was on to something.

Mike had thought his father's sympathy for stomach upset might save him. After all, the man was known to be toxic when he headed into the bathroom with the Sunday paper.

"Michael? Did you forget the question?" His mom was closing in; the seat was getting way too hot.

"I don't know."

"How can you not know?"

"Mom, come on. How am I supposed to know? He said he didn't feel good and that he'd already eaten."

Mike's dad chimed in, "So, you don't know specifically that he's sick from the food he ate?"

"No," Mike glumly responded.

His parents exchanged a knowing look. There was a pause in the action before the trump card was played. Mike was involuntarily holding his breath, bracing for the next question--the seconds ticked off as if attached to a bomb in his head.

"Well, I better get up there and check on him and make sure he's OK." Mrs. Dean started to get up from the table.

"No! I mean, you can't." Mike had the pleading look of the guilty.

His mom sat back down and leaned in to her son, "All right,

NEARFALL:

Michael Dean, let's hear the truth. You're already in deep water without a life vest, so you better come clean right now." Mike knew he was sunk.

For the next ten minutes, Mike spilled the beans. He told his parents about the Mill House, the pot, the girls, Dan skipping practice, and then showing up wasted on the doorstep. "I didn't know what to do. He was scared and said people were after him." Mike stopped to come up for air.

His parents sat back their chairs. His father spoke first. "Is that the whole truth?" Mike nodded yes. "Well, we're going to speak with your wrestling coach to make sure that you went to practice as you say you did." Mike's dad believed him. He just wanted to see whether there was anything Mike was leaving out. He threw in contacting the coach, because he knew that his son wouldn't want to jeopardize being able to wrestle.

"OK, but I told him that Dan was sick. Are you going to say anything about that?"

"Well, your mother and I are going to discuss that in a little bit. Right now, I'm going up to check on Dan."

Mike slumped in his chair, as his dad headed up the stairs. Matt who had been sitting silently during the last several minutes, was absolutely wide-eyed, and on the edge of his seat. He couldn't believe his ears. Here he was worrying about covering his tracks over a fight at school, and his brother has a buddy upstairs, boozed, stoned, and most likely, passed out. All of a sudden, Matt's problem seemed like a little tiny drizzle, while Mike's situation seemed like a massive thunderstorm with an impending tornado warning.

"Well, Big Brother, you sure know how to spice up dinner." Matt

Chapter Five

was reveling in his new lease on life. Unexpectedly, his burden had been lifted, and he couldn't resist poking a jab at Mike.

"Yeah, you're a real comedian, Mr. Rockem Sockem Robot." Mike raised an eyebrow to let Matt know that he still had the goods to bring his younger brother into the doghouse with him. Matt got the message, and his mocking grin quickly faded.

"Do you know why Dan thought people were chasing him?" His mother asked. Mike replied, "No."

Mrs. Dean looked at both her sons before explaining. "Marijuana makes some people really paranoid. They think someone is watching them or chasing them. It can be a very scary experience. So scary that there have been some people that have committed suicide because they felt the panic would never end. This is one of the many reasons I hope you boys will never smoke marijuana. Michael, I want you to know, and I think that I can speak for your father as well, we're proud of you for not caving in to the peer pressure. That was a big test in your life, and you passed. You made the right decision. There will be more situations to come. You'll face a lot more peer pressure in the months and years ahead. I can only hope that you'll continue to be strong like you were today. We know it's difficult when you're trying to fit in, and you want to be cool. But as you go from being boys to men, you'll learn that honest hard work and integrity are the best kind of cool."

Mike's mood had been brightening with his mother's praise, but that was brought to a screeching halt as the twinge of guilt hit him about cheating on the test.

"In the future I hope that you'll come to us and discuss these situations, instead of trying to hide them like you did tonight. Certainly, lying about it only makes matters worse."

NEARFALL:

The two boys glanced at one another, both knowing that it wasn't only Mike that had things to hide.

"I'm going to go up and see how your father is doing with Dan. You boys think about things while you clear the table and do the dishes. If you have any questions, we'll talk about them when I get back downstairs."

Mrs. Dean was on her way to the stairwell when the front door bell rang. "Now who could that be?" After the surprises of the evening, she braced herself for what might be next.

Mike's mind whirled. "Who could it be? Was it the police? Was it Dan's dad? Maybe their wrestling coach — but how would he have found out?"

Mrs. Dean opened the door...Standing in front of her was a pretty, bright-eyed young girl.

"Is Matt here?"

Mrs. Dean smiled, somewhat relieved. "Yes, he's here, but he's doing some chores right now. Isn't it a little late for you to be out?"

Kimberly cheerfully replied, "Oh I'm with friends. They're around the corner. We go for a walk after dinner with our moms for exercise. By the way, I'm Kimberly."

Mrs. Dean smiled warmly, "Well, it's very nice to meet you Kimberly. Would you like me to get Matt?"

Kimberly quickly said, "No, that's OK, Mrs. Dean. Could you just tell him that I stopped by?"

Mrs. Dean again smiled at the confidence of this young girl. "Yes,

Chapter Five

of course I'll tell him. Is there any message?"

Kimberly's assuredness broke momentarily as she blushed the way one does when they have a crush, but she quickly gathered herself. "Just tell him that I thought he was really brave today, the way he took on that big bully. I mean everybody in our grade, well almost the whole school, is afraid of TJ. It was just really cool, even if Matt didn't win."

Mrs. Dean looked at Kimberly for a moment, blinking in astonishment. "Well Kimberly, it certainly was a pleasure to meet you, and I'll be sure to tell him."

"Thanks, Mrs. Dean." Kimberly practically skipped down the sidewalk, obviously very happy with the message she delivered.

Mrs. Dean watched as Kimberly turned the corner out of sight and then shut the door. Her voice reached decibels seldom heard without a microphone. "MATTHEW PATRICK DEAN!!!!"

CHAPTER 6

Matt's back stiffened as his mother's shouted words vibrated through his body. The bowl he had been clearing from the table slipped from his hands and tumbled to the floor. The hair on the back of his neck snapped to attention. Matt knew from the sound and the force of hearing his full name that his mother was onto him—he knew it in an instant. His mother so rarely yelled that, when she did, you knew that there was nowhere to hide and nowhere to run. Michael looked at his brother with pity; he knew there was no saving him. Matt's only thought, as the sound of his mother's steps drew closer, was "This is really going to suck."

So began another round of white hot interrogation and confession. Matt's dad, having heard his wife's battle cry, quickly joined the fray. His checking on Dan was already complete—actually there wasn't much to it. Dan was passed out on the bathroom floor.

After making sure he was breathing OK and not choking on his tongue, Mr. Dean just tried to make Dan comfortable. The bathroom floor was tile and tended to be rather cold. He had thought about putting Dan into a bed, but figured there was a high degree of likelihood that Dan would need to be very close to the toilet the next several hours. In the end, Mr. Dean simply placed a pillow under Dan's head and covered him with a blanket. He had just put the blanket over Dan when he heard his wife's call to arms.

The first "incident" with Mike had tested their patience. The conspiracy with Matt tipped the apple cart. Mike was sucked back in, because he knew the truth about what happened with Matt and helped conceal it. When it was all over and the smoke cleared—Final score: Parents 65 Dean boys 0. It was a shut out. The Dean brothers not only didn't win a match, they didn't so much as get a takedown or an escape in the entire discussion with their parents. Actually, "discussion" is probably too generous a term, unless of course, one would view the conversation between a Marine Corps drill instructor and some new recruits as a "discussion."

Ultimately, calm prevailed, and, to be fair, Mom and Dad Dean didn't really yell…much. It wasn't the crimes themselves, but the active attempt to cover up and lie about the incidents that really got the boys in hot water. The punishments were handed out without ceremony. They were both to be grounded two weeks—no TV, no computer, no video games, and there would be extra chores for the next two Saturdays. Mike and Matt apologized, and trudged off to bed.

Mr. Dean looked over his shoulder as the "prisoners" plodded up the staircase behind him. He could see them through the large doorway between the living room and the front door. He gave them one last stern "Good night, Boys." Matt sullenly replied, "Night." As if "goodnight" would be too optimistic.

Michael was following behind Matt and meekly waved. As their legs and feet gradually disappeared to the upstairs, Mr. Dean leaned forward, and picked up the newspaper from the coffee table. He casually fell back in his chair and glanced at his wife before fixing his gaze on the headlines. "So, anything new happen today, Dear?" Mrs. Dean burst out with a laugh, but quickly covered her mouth, so that the boys didn't hear her. Regaining composure she added, "No, actually, it's been rather dull today—just the same old, same old. Anything new with you?" Mr. Dean's expression was one of deep contemplation as if trying to recall something of significance. "Nope, nothing that I can think of."

After years of parenting a couple of high energy boys, they had learned to take most things in stride. Mrs. Dean suggested, "Why don't I heat up the rest of your dinner and make some fresh coffee, then we can talk about what to do next."

"Hmmm, a quiet late dinner with my wife, that sounds nice-- whatever would we find to talk about?" he asked mockingly.

Mike spit his toothpaste into the sink. Matt was already in bed staring at the ceiling. Mike rinsed his mouth out and ran the toothbrush under the water before dropping it into the ceramic Mickey Mouse toothbrush holder—the same one he had had since he was six years old. The thought dashed through his mind that he was probably a little too old for a Mickey Mouse toothbrush holder, "Maybe the Iowa Hawkeyes or the Green Bay Packers have one I could buy?" That sounded more grown up. He made a mental note to make the appropriate update.

Mike stepped over Dan who was still asleep on the floor and snoring loudly. "Better leave the fan on to drown out that walrus, or I'll never get to sleep." Mike snapped off the bathroom light and made his way into the bedroom. Matt had already shut the bedroom light off, forcing Mike to navigate the mine field. "Why the heck did you already shut the light off?" Matt didn't respond. He just continued looking at the ceiling.

Chapter Six

Within seconds, Mike stubbed his toe on the weights that he had recently purchased with his allowance. "Son of a....gun!"

Matt quietly smiled. "Ah, the small victories of the younger brother."

Matt would sometimes mess around with the weights too, but usually just to mock Mike—grunting and straining the way Mike would when he got tired. For some reason, the dumbbells found their way to the middle of the room with the lights off no less. Despite the seriousness of the evening, Matt just couldn't completely stifle his mischievous nature.

With Mike still hopping around on one foot, the glory of the moment quickly faded as Matt's thoughts drifted back to his punishment. Mike was muttering something under his breath as he crawled into bed. "Probably curse words," Matt thought.

Mike exhaled as the pain started to subside. It hadn't dawned on him that his brother would have chosen this particular moment to sabotage him. In Mike's way of thinking, it was the equivalent of running a combat drill on a submarine, in the middle of a galley fire. For Matt, it was payback for the atomic wedgie...from six months ago. Matt apparently had embraced the philosophy that revenge is a dish best served cold.

"I don't see why I got the same punishment as you. I'm not the one with a drunk passed out in our bathroom. I don't see where getting my head kicked in is on the same level. Where's the sympathy—I'm not even going to get any cash for this tooth knocked out of my mouth!"

Mike responded as he thought his parents would, "Well, I'm pretty sure you are not being punished for getting in a fight; I think it has more to do with the fact that you lied about it. I think that came across loud and clear during the lecture."

"Yeah, but my lie didn't involve illegal substances. I just don't think I should have gotten two weeks."

Matt crossed his arms on his chest in defiance. Mike offered his brother an option. "Well, I dare you to go back downstairs and tell Mom and Dad that. I'm sure they'll be real open to your point of view."

Matt thought about it for a couple seconds and reached his final answer, "No way! I'm not going back down there."

Mike bunched up his pillow and rolled to his side. "Well, then shut up, and go to sleep."

Mr. and Mrs. Dean had gone back into the kitchen and were drinking their coffee. Mr. Dean's straight black as always and Mrs. Dean's more milk and sugar than coffee. "So, what do you want to do about Dan? You and I have long suspected that he's been abused, and, if what Mike is saying is true, this could really be a bad scene." Mrs. Dean looked at her husband as he pondered his reply.

"Well, I gotta tell you Hon, there's a part of me that thinks he needs is good butt-whupping for a stunt like this."

"Yeah, but come on, Peter, you and I know that your definition of a spanking and some elevated anger, is considerably different than being beaten with a pipe or smacked in the face with a closed fist. That's what this kid is most likely to receive when he gets home—that is if we make the phone call. Myself, I think we should call Child Protective Services."

Mr. Dean looked up at his wife like she had taken leave of her senses. "No, we're not doing that. Dan will never admit any wrong doing by his father, and we can't prove any abuse. Even if we could, I'm not sure taking him out of the home is the best thing for him. He's learned to stay out of his dad's way by now, and he's over here nearly as much as he's at home. I think we should encourage that as much as possible. However, we are definitely going to have a heart-to-heart with Danny boy when he sobers up. And I already have some jobs he's going to help me with in the garage—he's going to get some work piled on him, same as Mike and Matt."

Mrs. Dean contemplated her husband's response. "Speaking of work, how did the job interview go?"

Mr. Dean took another sip of his jet black coffee. "It went well. I have another interview with the plant manager tomorrow. I'm pretty sure that I'll get the job. It's a thirty-mile drive each way, but hey, it's a good company, and it seems like there might be a chance to advance quickly."

Mrs. Dean exhaled, "That's a relief. I've been on pins and needles all day—Lord knows we could use the money."

For a moment the conversation fell quiet; unspoken tension hung in the air. Mrs. Dean wished she could reel back in what she had just said. Her husband was well aware they needed money. He certainly didn't need the reminder, and it wasn't going to help his interview tomorrow to add any additional pressure.

"Well, I mean if Dan is going to be a more frequent house guest, you may need to get a second job and I'll have to start having bake sales. That boy eats as though he has a hollow leg."

Mr. Dean smiled at his wife's attempt to make him feel better. "Yeah, he's got a healthy appetite, but he's going to be a big guy. His dad is a big guy. Are you planning to call the school about this TJ kid?"

NEARFALL:

Mrs. Dean nodded in the affirmative as she took a bite of an oatmeal raisin cookie.

"Well, I'd like you to hold off on that for a little bit—let's see if this behavior continues. I'm curious to see how this plays out." Mr. Dean gave his wife a little wink.

Mike's bed was closest to the window, and Matt's was closest to the door. Mike had been lobbying for his own room for quite a while, and certainly Matt wasn't protesting such a change. However, with their dad getting laid off, creative money sources were being considered. The Dean home, though modest, somehow managed to squeeze in four small bedrooms—one for the kids, one for the parents, a guest room where their grandparents stayed nearly every weekend, and one room that was really a den/office.

Mr. Dean had been working on the den in the evening and weekends. He was remodeling it, and putting in a separate entryway so that it could be leased out. So, for the foreseeable future, Mike and Matt were stuck with each other.

"Hey, you still awake?" Mike asked.

"Yeah, but aren't you the one that told me to shut up and go to sleep?"

Mike looked over at Matt. Their eyes had adjusted to the dark and they could see gray outlines of one another. "So it seems that Mattie's little girlfriend likes him too."

Matt was puzzled by this read of the situation. "I doubt it. She probably thinks I'm the biggest dork ever. That's why she couldn't wait to rat me out."

Mike discharged such notions, "Nah, come on, chicks don't come

47

Chapter Six

to the house of guys they don't like."

"Really?" Matt's voice cracked with a youthful squeal, "I mean, really?"

Mike propped himself up on his elbow. "Yeah, of course—think about it, would you stop by the house of some girl you didn't like or thought was a goober?"

Matt deliberated for a moment. "Well, maybe if I was hoping to get her in trouble."

Mike shook his head. "No way. You wouldn't waste your time."

Matthew was encouraged. "Hmmm, I hadn't thought of it like that."

All of a sudden going back to school didn't seem as horrible as it did just a few minutes earlier. Matt had instant butterflies. "Hey, thanks, Mike. I was sorta hating the idea of going back to school, but maybe you're right. Maybe I've got something to look forward to."

Mike's generosity had its limits. "Sure, no problem—but just because your little chickadee doesn't think you're a dork, doesn't mean I don't."

Matt wasn't fazed in the least. "Yeah, whatever."

After a prolonged silence, Matt's excitement started to wane. The realization that he was possibly the object of Kimberly's affection, didn't change the fact that TJ was still lurking to squash any potential romance before it even had a chance to bloom.

"Hey, Mike, you're still going to teach me to wrestle, right?"
Mike nodded in the darkness, "Yeah, I know what you're think-

ing…I'll talk to my coach. I have a feeling I'm going to be forced to talk to him anyhow."

Matthew sympathized with his brother's situation. "It looks like we both need to face the music when we get back to school. Goodnight, Mike."

"Goodnight, Matt."

Mike rolled over again to gaze out the window. The moon was nearly full, and Mike could see a raccoon making its way across the yard—his bandit-like mask hiding his true identity. "Probably stole some of the trash again," Mike thought. "No wonder he wears a mask and does his work at night." With all the commotion regarding Dan and Matt, there was one big thing that hadn't completely escaped his thought—the test he cheated on.

Mike was getting the test back tomorrow, and the anxiety was twofold—if he didn't pass, he was off the wrestling team. That was bad enough, but, for all the talk of honesty from his parents this evening, Mike was still harboring a secret—he stole the answers to that test. Mike again looked at the raccoon as the thief was waddling down the sidewalk. "Maybe I should wear a mask too." Dreading the morning, Mike closed his eyes and tried to sleep away his guilt.

CHAPTER 7

Dan's head was pounding, and he could see red. It was as though the hammer in his head was smashing a tomato with such force that it covered his eyes. Every pump of his pulse sent the anvil through his skull. A far away voice was becoming more audible. "Dan, get up. It's time to get going, Son". The gruff, early morning voice of Mr. Dean was accompanied by a foot, gently, and then not so gently, nudging him awake. Dan opened his eyes to find himself laid out on the bathroom floor, eyeball level, with the base of the toilet. It became apparent that the "squishing tomato" was Mr. Dean flicking the light on and off. And what Dan was really seeing was the back of his own eyelids. Mr. Dean slurped a drink of black coffee, the smell of which was making Dan immediately nauseated.

Dan was having trouble focusing his eyes and would close them for a few seconds at a time to get relief.

"How are you feeling?" Mr. Dean had a pretty good idea, but it seemed like the right question to ask.

NEARFALL:

Dan gathered himself before answering, "I feel like a big turd. What happened?"

Mr. Dean was slightly amused by the answer. "Well, you don't look so great either. You came over here last night bombed, and then passed out in the boys' bathroom."

Despite how awful Dan felt, he could still feel the sting of embarrassment and the angst of guilt. "I'm sorry about that, Mr. Dean."

Mr. Dean tried not to show much in the way of sympathy, and he certainly projected enough authority so that Dan knew there were going to be consequences. Sorry alone wasn't going to cut it. "Well, you get yourself into the shower and get cleaned up. Mike set some clothes out for you on the bed, and there are some eggs for you downstairs, OK?" Dan's eyes had closed again, and Mr. Dean wasn't certain that Dan was altogether in the here and now. "OK?" he repeated.

Dan nodded his head in the affirmative but was really just trying to keep from throwing up. The mere mention of the eggs had his tonsils floating. Mr. Dean turned to go. "I'm going to leave the light on. You've got 15 minutes to get ready and be downstairs. The train is pulling out in 40 minutes. You got me?" Dan again nodded, and a satisfied Mr. Dean left the room.

The jackhammer in Dan's head was unrelenting. His mouth tasted and felt like a cat had used it for a litter box. He pulled himself to his knees and waited a few seconds for the room to stop spinning. He put his right elbow and forearm on the toilet seat and pulled his head over the bowl...he was going to puke. He just knew it. A minute went by, and nothing happened, but the puke feeling was right there at the back of his throat. It was so awful he wished he could just throw up to get it over with.

Chapter Seven

Dan ran his hand through his hair. It was as though his head was three feet thick, and he hadn't slept in a week. "Oh, dear God…Why did I drink that stuff?" He groaned as he tried to pull himself to a standing position, his left hand on the wall and his right pushing up on the bathroom sink.

He made it to his feet but fell against the wall for support. The tile was cool and felt comforting against his skin. A sweat had broken out as though he had a fever. Everything was excruciating. The light was so bright. The hum of the bathroom fan was like standing near the engines of a 747 jumbo jet. Mr. Dean's voice thundered from downstairs, "Nine minutes, Dan!"

Dan struggled with the shower door. "How could six minutes have already passed? I'm never gonna make it". As the water came crashing down, Dan got undressed and hopped in. "WHOA!!!" he yelped. In his hangover haze, he'd forgotten to turn on the hot water. He danced, jumped, and flailed frantically, as he attempted to grab the hot water knob. Fortunately for Dan, the hot water soon kicked in. He finally settled at luke warm.

On the upside, the cold water seemed to jolt him a bit closer to actually being awake. He let the water run down his face, as his bearings started coming back. The pickled brain that was stuck between his ears, somewhere near park or neutral, started to crackle to life.

As it did, panic began to set in. "Does my dad know? Did the Deans call him? Are they going to tell the school and my coach?" But that wasn't his biggest worry. "How am I going to face Mr. and Mrs. Dean? Dan worried that this huge screw-up might be the end of his relationship with the Deans. And that scared him more than anything, more than school suspension, his coach's discipline or his father's rage. The Deans were his safety net, and he needed them. Nervous knots of anxiety teamed up with his already nauseous stomach. "What have I done? I'm so screwed."

Mr. Dean looked at his watch in between bites of toast. "Do you think I should go back up there?"

Mrs. Dean paused for a moment and cocked her head to the side. "No, I can hear the shower running."

Mr. Dean crinkled up his face. "How the heck can you hear that?"

She smiled sweetly. "I'm not hard of hearing like you."

He waved her off. "You've been saying that for fifteen years. There's nothing wrong with my hearing."

"What's that, Dear? I'm sorry. Could you repeat that?" Mrs. Dean teased.

"I said there's nothing wrong with my hearing. I just can't hear the earthworms moving under my feet like some people I know." Mr. Dean seemed pleased with his rebuttal.

Matt and Mike had been sitting silently through breakfast as they watched the drama unfold with Dan. They had already gotten their punishment last night, so, for the moment, they decided to go with the old saying, "Children should be seen and not heard." It was definitely in their best interest to keep a low profile and avoid getting caught in any crossfire. However, Matt couldn't contain himself anymore and broke ranks. "Our teacher was saying that girls can hear better than boys." Mike shot him a "What the heck are you doing?" look followed by a quick shake of the head "NO".

Mrs. Dean looked at Matt and said "I think you'll find that girls do most things better than boys."

Chapter Seven

Mr. Dean leaned into Matt, "It's OK to let them think that, it's easier that way." Mr. Dean gave his boys a little wink and Mrs. Dean rolled her eyes.

Matt and Mike were used to this type of chitchat from their parents. It was part of their charm—they loved teasing each other. When he was younger, Mike worried that other people might think his parents were arguing, but over time he could see it was fairly obvious that it was all in good fun.

Matt continued with his reckless open mouth. "Where you headed today, Pops?"

Mr. Dean eyed him incredulously. "Pops? Who are you calling Pops? Let's stick with Dad, Father or better yet, Sir."

Mike let his guard down and spoke as a reflex, "Sir? Since when have we ever called you Sir?"

Mrs. Dean was packing lunches for school. "How about, 'Overlord'?"

Mr. Dean ignored his wife and took a bead on Mike, pointing a finger in his direction, "For all the commotion you've caused in the last 24 hours, you should be happy I let you eat, let alone speak."

Mike sank back into his chair. "Yes Sir."

Mike wanted to throw a flag, and ask for an instant replay. After all, why didn't Matt get scorned for speaking up?

Mr. Dean noticed the "that's unfair" look in Mike's eyes and redirected his finger at Matt. "That goes for you too Buddy." Mr. Dean continued, "Now, to answer your question, I'm wearing a sport coat and tie, because I have a final interview today, and I hope to be returning home with a new job."

Mr. Dean got up to put his dirty dishes in the sink. Matt piped up, "If you get the job, I'll call you Overlord."

Mrs. Dean gave her husband a kiss on the cheek, "You'll get it, Honey. And when you do, I might be willing to call you Overlord too...at least for an evening."

Mr. Dean put an arm around his wife's waist and pulled her to him. He gave her a kiss on the lips that was more than just their usual peck.

This received an immediate reaction from Matt. "Eww, that's gross. You guys are sick."

Mrs. Dean looked at Matt. "You wouldn't think it was sick if it was that little Kimberly girl that was at the door last night."

Matt stammered and stuttered, "What do you mean?" Mike burst out laughing. His brother's face and neck were beet, beet red.

Mr. Dean tussled Matt's hair. "It's OK, Kiddo. Your Mom tells me she's pretty cute."

Dan sat on the steps listening to the happy sounds of the Dean family. He wondered if today would be the last day he'd be part of it. He was still massively queasy and rested his head against the handrail. "Well, here goes nothing." Dan pulled himself to his feet and started to make his way downstairs.

"Shh." Mrs. Dean was listening to something. With a hushed voice she turned to her kids, "Guys, Dan's coming down...Do you really want to be here?"

Chapter Seven

Matt and Mike immediately pushed back their chairs, grabbed their lunches, and ran for the front door. "Bye Mom, bye Dad." As they whisked past the landing of the stairwell, Dan was rounding the corner. "Good luck, Dude. We'll be outside." Dan watched the door slam shut behind them and exhaled heavily.

Mr. and Mrs. Dean looked at each other as Mr. Dean walked over to the fridge. "You ready?"

Mrs. Dean nodded and made a beeline toward Dan. They were about to initiate some aversion therapy for young Daniel. Dan's slow shuffle came to an abrupt stop as he noticed Mrs. Dean's rapid progress in his direction. She immediately started in on him, talking fast, loud, high energy and not waiting for input from Dan. "Well, Daniel, how are you feeling this morning? I see you managed to get some clothes on, although you're looking a little green around the gills. Let's get right at it, shall we?" She grabbed Dan by the arm and pulled him into the living room.

"No sense beating around the bush. Your punishment starts immediately." She thrust the vacuum cleaner handle into his hand. "I need the downstairs done before you leave for school." With that, she turned it on, and gave him a little push forward.

The noise was deafening. Dan was holding his stomach and the vacuum, but he really needed a third hand to hold his head which felt like it was about to explode. Dan hadn't even completed a five-foot by five-foot section of the carpet, when Mr. Dean came bounding into his line of sight. With the vacuum running, Mr. Dean pulled a beer out from behind his back. Dan thought he was delusional, because he wasn't aware that Mr. Dean even drank beer. He watched as Mr. Dean cracked it open, and then yelled over the vacuum that it would help with the hangover if Dan took a BIG whiff of the smell. Mr. Dean held the can out in front of Dan who leaned in and inhaled deeply....That was it....game over. The gears in his stomach hit reverse mode, and Dan dropped the vacuum and dashed for the kitchen sink. He made it, but just barely, the vomit splattered over the freshly washed and rinsed dishes.

Mrs. Dean, who had been waiting for him in the kitchen, turned her head from the foul smell and wrinkled her noise. She pulled the sprayer out, and turned on the water. "Clean that up, and here's a toothbrush and toothpaste. Put the dishes in the dishwasher, and come out to the living room when you're finished."

Dan emerged a few minutes later. Seated in the two chairs opposite the couch were Mr. and Mrs. Dean. Dan dutifully took the couch and braced for the worst. "Do you feel a little better?" Dan nodded yes.

Mr. Dean leaned forward and looked at his watch. "We don't have a lot of time right now, but here's the long and short of it. We're deeply disappointed in you. Dan, you know better. Now, here's how this is going to play out. For now, we're not going to tell the school, or your coach. However, you're going to be helping me in the shop for the next couple of Saturdays, and you're going to be staying here as much as you can this week while you work off a list of chores that we've prepared for you. I know you need to work it around your father, but if you fail to show up or fail to complete the tasks, we'll make the call to the school and your coach."

Mrs. Dean looked at Dan. "Daniel, you must know that Mr. Dean and I are very fond of you. We love having you as a part of our extended family, but you also need to know that this behavior is unacceptable. Do you understand that?"

Dan's eyes welled up with tears. He was embarrassed and ashamed, but mostly he was just so happy that they were willing

Chapter Seven

to give him another chance. "Yes, I understand, and I'm so sorry. It won't happen again."

Mr. Dean looked at his watch again. "OK, I've got to get you boys to school, so that will have to be it for now. We'll talk more later. Oh, one last thing—I'd eat light for lunch. Later today I'll be placing a call to your wrestling coach, letting him know how you and Mike were mocking how easy practice was becoming for you and how you barely get tired anymore, it's such a breeze."

"Oh no," Dan thought. Their coach was a guy that prided himself on conditioning; he was constantly talking about "outworking the competition." This was exactly the type of challenge he would really gear up for—a couple of cocky kids mouthing off about how easy his practices had become. Wrestling practice was going to be brutal.

Dan emerged from the house to join Matt and Mike outside.

"How did it go?" Mike asked.

"How do you think it went?" Dan replied.

The three boys waited in silence for Mr. Dean, each contemplating what the day held in store for them: Matt, not knowing if he'd be the dork of the 4th grade after getting his head kicked in; Mike, worried about the outcome of the test he'd cheated on; and Dan, trying to figure out how he was going to survive practice with a wicked hangover.

Mr. Dean opened the front door. "All right boys, let's go face the firing squad." Unknown to the boys, it was probably Mr. Dean who was more nervous than any of them...He really needed this job.

CHAPTER 8

Mr. Dean was going over in his head the things he wanted to say at this interview. The drive to the plant was a familiar one; he had been down this stretch of highway countless times in his life. Having grown up in the area, Mr. Dean knew every rise and every curve in the road. There was a certain comfort that came from knowing the route; it allowed his mind to focus on this final meeting. "What do I need to say to seal the deal?" As he neared the turnoff to the factory, the cornfield-lined highway wound on to the horizon, and the muted morning light was giving way to the brilliance of a cloudless sun.

He tried to anticipate what questions they might ask and rehearsed his answers before pulling into the company parking lot. It annoyed him that he had been out of work for so many months. He wanted to provide a secure home for his wife and kids. They were his life and his reason for getting up everyday. If he could pass the test today, this new position would be a good job with decent pay and a chance for advancement. Although he had never worked in window manufacturing he hoped his years of experience in different manufacturing processes would be helpful.

Chapter Eight

Certainly, it had gotten him this far in the interview process.

The car was still idling as he checked himself in the rearview mirror. He had a thinning crop of light brown hair that he parted to the side. It wasn't quite a comb-over, but he knew it was eventually heading in that direction. He patted his hair down and brushed it over with his hand. He looked for ear wax and nose hair…none to be found. Mr. Dean took a deep breath, straightened his tie and opened the car door.

Meanwhile, Matt was taking the walk to his classroom. He was running a little late, so most, if not all, of his classmates were already in the room. "OK, Fellow 4th Graders, say hello to the biggest weenie in the history of grade school. Hi, I'm Matt Dean please feel free to use me as a punching bag." The swelling had gone down some overnight, but he was still badly bruised. Like father, like son, he took a deep breath and opened the door.

As the door swung open and Matt stepped in the room, all eyes turned as if drawn like bugs to the light. Just as he feared, Matt was the center of attention in the worst way possible. "Why don't I make the humiliation complete, and just announce that I still wet the bed?" Matt didn't actually wet the bed anymore but felt that his current plight was on par with soaking the sheets.

Matt made his way to his desk while looking at the floor tile. He wished he could come up with a good reason to turn right back around and head for home. He swung himself into his chair and propped up his purpled face with his hands. He passed the first intolerable seconds staring at some stupid carving in the desk top that was probably made 20 years prior. "Jim luvs Wendy." "I wonder who Wendy was," Matt thought. "I wonder if she was a hottie like Kimberly." Ah yes, Kimberly, the girl that had gotten him into this whole mess. No way was he even going to glance in her direction.

And then a funny thing happened. The kid behind him, Luke Hunter, was tapping him on the back. Luke was a nice enough guy and they had some laughs together at recess but Matt didn't want to hear the ribbing that Luke was surely going to throw his way. Matt ignored Luke's tap. Luke waited for a few seconds and then tapped again, this time more insistently. Matt gave a glance at his teacher, Mrs. Wilson, who was conducting roll call, to make sure he had an opening.

He turned in his seat slightly. "What do you want?"

Luke smiled. "Dude, I just wanted to be the first to shake your hand. Way to go man. You stood up to that blowhard!"

Matt was shocked by the sentiment. All he could muster was, "Thanks." But, before he could spin back around, Barry in the next row over leaned over and threw his two cents in. "Good job," he said as he reached out to shake Matt's hand. Matt looked up and let his eyes dart around the room; there were a bunch of kids looking in his direction. Not with scorn, but something more like admiration. Matt turned back in his seat. "Wow, this is strange." Matt stole a glance in Kimberly's direction. There she was—looking right at him in all her radiance and giving him the biggest smile that any 10 year old boy could ever hope for...

Mr. Dean pulled open the glass door at the entrance of the company headquarters. Stepping up to the receptionist's desk he introduced himself. "Hi, I'm Peter Dean. I have an appointment to meet Jack Ross."

While Mike's dad took a chair, Mike was also seated awaiting his fate. Mr. Rhenkin was passing out the tests. Mike was on pins and needles not only to find out if he passed, but mostly to see if he got busted for cheating. The gut ache from the worry alone was definitely not worth it. Mr. Rhenkin, in his fetching yellow, "Hi,

I'm a moron" bow tie, was working his way down the row, efficiently passing the tests back to both his right and left. "I wonder how he organized it so that he could pull that off? We're seated alphabetically. Did he actually take the time to alternately mix the rows? Why not just pass it out by row?" Mike shook his head. "It's weird the things you think when you're nervous."

Mike glanced over at Billy Johnson's grade as Mr. Rhenkin handed the test back to him. Billy's brow furrowed as he looked at the paper. He seemed disappointed. "Oh, oh." Mike thought, "Maybe I bet on the wrong horse." Billy sat back in his seat and revealed the grade, B+. Part of Mike silently celebrated—based on Billy's grade it seemed as though Mike would at least get a C. Now for the bigger question of whether he would get sent to the gallows for cheating. Mr. Rhenkin handed Mike his test. "Nice job, Mike." Mike looked down at his grade, A-. He couldn't believe it. Mike flipped to the back page where he simply went from multiple choice to multiple guess, writing ABCD randomly just to finish the test. Unbelievably, he had gotten all but one of them right.

Mike looked up to see Billy just seething. Billy's hand shot up in the air as Mr. Rhenkin was working his way back to the front of the room on the next set of rows. "Oh crap! He's going to rat me out." Mr. Rhenkin had his back to Billy, but it would be only seconds before Billy's raised hand came into his field of vision. Mike tried desperately to get Billy's attention…

Mr. Dean sat with his back straight against the chair and his hands neatly folded in his lap. He noticed a couple of pieces of lint on the front of his pants and peeled them away. It was a small thing, and certainly it shouldn't be the difference between getting the job and not, but it kept his mind busy. He was a big believer in doing the little things right. Besides, at this point he had no idea what might make the difference in getting the job. Would the boss believe that a guy with lint all over his pants could be the person to improve quality and shave minutes off the manufacturing process? He didn't know, but he wasn't taking any chances.

"Mr. Ross will see you now. You can go into Conference Room 2. It's down the hall and on your left." The receptionist gave him a little smile. She was an older woman, and maybe she could see on his face that he really needed this job. "Good luck," she offered. Mr. Dean smiled back and responded with a warm "Thank you." He was happy for any well-wishers he could get.

The conference room was pretty sparse. Nothing but a long mahogany table surrounded by comfortable looking chairs, a phone and a white board for those markers that you can erase. Mr. Dean took a seat. There was one picture in the room, and it was directly across from him. It was of the Iowa Hawkeye wrestling team holding one of their many National Championship trophies. The caption said, "They can, because they believe they can." "Mike would like that," Mr. Dean thought to himself. Mr. Ross breezed into the room just at that moment.

"I'm sorry to have kept you waiting, Peter." Mr. Ross plopped down in the chair at the end of the table.

"Not a problem at all, Mr. Ross."

"Please, call me Jack," Mr. Ross replied.

Mr. Ross had his head down reviewing his notes. His movements were quick, and he seemed to be a man on the go. He was tall with silver hair, but very casually dressed for a senior level executive. He had dress slacks and a dress shirt, but the sleeves were rolled up, and he wasn't wearing a tie.

"Well, Peter, I have to tell you that in the reports that I've received, everyone is very impressed with you. So I just have a couple of questions."

Dan had been resting his head on the desk trying to be as still as possible, hoping that might quiet the thunder going off in his melon. But when he received his test, he kept his head up, and waited for Mike to get his test back. That way they could console one another, as they basked in their academic failure. Dan held up his end of the bargain. He posted a solid D on the test. But, as he looked over in Mike's direction, he realized something had gone horribly wrong. He knew Mike had cheated and had been worried about it. Now, seeing Billy's hand in the air and Mike begging him to relent, Dan knew Mike required some assistance…he needed a diversion.

Dan jumped out his seat, spinning wildly toward the front of the room, shouting, "Get it off me! Get it off me!" He clutched at his clothes and tried to shake off whatever it was that was on him. "I can't get it off! I don't want it to go down my pants!" Dan was now ripping off his T-shirt standing in the front of the room. Mr. Rhenkin and the rest of the class were watching in utter amazement.

Mike used the opening to jump out his seat and sidled up to Billy. Mike was crouched down out of Mr. Rhenkin's view. "Come on, Man. Don't do this — I'll do anything. What do you want?"

Billy looked at the desperation in Mike's eyes. He knew he had him and could blackmail Mike for anything. "All right, but you're going to pay for my silence."

Mike glanced up at Dan. His buddy's antics were rapidly coming to a close. "OK — anything. Anything you want. You got it."

Mike jumped back to his seat just as Dan stomped several times with his foot emphatically "killing" whatever it was that had been "crawling" on him. Dan sheepishly looked at Mr. Rhenkin. "I'm kinda afraid of spiders." Mr. Rhenkin sighed, the pained sigh of an intellectual having to deal with morons. "Well, at least I know you're not dead. Before that display of yours, I wasn't quite sure. Could you please put your shirt back on and take your seat?"

As Dan walked back to his desk he gave a quick flex and wink to Vanessa, the girl of interest on Dan's side of the room. She rolled her eyes and ignored him but then turned and smiled faintly to one of her girlfriends. Dan slid into his chair and looked over at Mike. Mike gave him a thumbs up and nod. Dan nodded back as if to say, "OK. Cool." Dan pulled his shirt back on; his insect performance sapped whatever reserves of energy he had. He looked down at his hands. They were shaking.

Matt was really starting to enjoy his newfound celebrity status. Apparently he had really turned a corner with Kimberly. Her secret fondness for Matt found full expression as if he had done battle for her honor and her heart. She had already covertly sent a note through the ranks that said she would like to see him after school. Matt thought, "Who knew so much could be accomplished by getting walloped in a fight?" And just when Matt was starting to warm up his pen for autographs and get out his Hollywood shades, Mr. Merrill, the principal, walked into the room. A hush fell over the class and all eyes went to Matt. "Mrs. Wilson, I'd like to see Matt Dean for a moment if I could." Matt rose from his chair. "Oh, oh. This could be bad."

After asking Mr. Dean a few questions about his family and how he likes living in Iowa, Mr. Ross was winding up his interview. "Peter, I know you came from a union shop, and by now I'm sure you're aware that our work force has chosen not to form a union. So I'm wondering how you feel about the relationship between management and labor?"

Chapter Eight

Mr. Dean leaned in and responded immediately, "My personal feeling is that there shouldn't be any division between the labor and management. There needs to be a feeling fostered that we're all in this together—not just in slogans, but in reality, and that includes allowing workers more responsibility and input in the decision-making process.

Along that line there needs to be some form of profit sharing so that everyone feels that if they go the extra mile, there's a reward beyond just being employed. But, with that there have to be expectations and goals. It's not a free lunch or extra benefit. It should be everybody working together while individually giving their best for a common goal. Just like that picture up there."

Mr. Ross looked up at the Iowa Wrestling National Championship Team and smiled. Mr. Dean knew there was some risk in what he was saying. There were a lot of companies that didn't want to eat into their profits by throwing in with the workers.

Mr. Ross leaned back in chair. "Well, Peter, that's why we're giving you this job." He stood up and stuck out his hand. "Welcome aboard."

Mr. Dean gave a vigorous handshake and couldn't contain his grin. "Thanks a lot, Jack. I can't wait to get started."

Mr. Ross turned to leave. "Feel free to use the phone in here, and, when you're done, there'll be some paperwork out front for you to fill out to make things official. Come back tomorrow, and we'll get started with a full orientation. I'm betting you'd like to call your wife now?" Mr. Dean's smile said it all. "By the way, that was a heck of an answer you gave."

"Thanks. It sounded even better in here than it did in my head out in the parking lot."

NEARFALL:

Mr. Ross laughed and ducked out the door.

Mr. Dean dialed as fast as his fingers would allow. He stood pacing waiting for Mrs. Dean to pick up. Finally after four rings, she answered. "Hello."

Mr. Dean couldn't wait an instant longer. "Hey, Hon, it's me…we got it!"

Mrs. Dean pumped her fist and did a little happy dance, but then very calmly replied, "Ah, Honey, that's great. I knew you'd get it."

The drive home was a much different experience than the one a couple of hours earlier. The paperwork that had to be filled out was extensive, but he was so happy that he scarcely even noticed. He couldn't wait to get home and see his wife. They had experienced so many ups and downs that it always seemed more meaningful when something good happened—especially when he could share it with her. Mr. Dean had the radio on, the window cracked to feel the rushing air, and was practically dancing in his seat.

He didn't see the deer immediately; it was grazing with its head down on a bit of an embankment. Mornings weren't usually their most active time. Dusk always seemed like the time when you really had to watch out for them, but, for whatever reason, something spooked the big buck, and the deer bolted. Mr. Dean noticed a flash of brown and swerved hard to the right to avoid the collision. His right front tire went off the shoulder and caught the edge of the embankment. Mr. Dean frantically tried to bring the car back to the left and slammed on the brakes, but it was too late, the loose rock of the shoulder didn't provide enough traction to stop. The car careened down the hill, flipping over and over before coming to rest on its roof at the bottom of the gulley.

Radiator fluid spilled onto the hot engine, giving off a sweet, sick odor, and the tires were still rotating as a half conscious Mr. Dean tried to assess the situation. He was disoriented and hanging upside down in his seat belt. Blood was pouring down his face, apparently from a large gash on his chin, and his right leg was pinned under the dash. Mr. Dean kicked at the dash with his left leg trying to free the trapped limb. He couldn't see how badly it was injured, but from the searing pain he had a pretty good idea it was broken. He tried to lean back and collect his breath, but he was having a hard time breathing deeply. "OK, just calm down and think. You're alive, that's a start. OK, now I just have to catch my breath." Mr. Dean thought about his wife and his two boys…no way was he going to leave them. He just needed to calm his labored breathing. He inhaled as deeply as he could. "That's not good," he thought. The odor was unmistakable…gasoline!

CHAPTER 9

"If there was ever an example of needing one of those new cell phones, this is it," Mr. Dean thought as his mind frantically grasped for solutions. He closed his eyes. The pain was increasingly difficult to ignore, and his breathing was becoming raspy with fluid. "How is anyone going to see me at the bottom of this hill?" He knew that cars very rarely exploded like they do in the movies, but with gasoline leaking, cars could certainly catch fire—and that didn't sound too appealing considering his current situation. Adding insult to injury, he didn't know how much time he had before he either passed out or the car ignited. He opened his eyes and again began kicking the crushed dashboard encased around his trapped leg. Every kick delivered screaming pain from his mangled limb. He felt himself becoming dizzy; he paused to survey his progress and rest. Mr. Dean had managed to move the dashboard a fair amount, and he tried to move his leg, but it didn't budge. "No more breaks," he thought and resumed kicking. It was his only option.

The hallway was empty and quiet. Matt closed the door behind him so the rest of the class couldn't see or hear what was being discussed. Matt looked up at his principal. Mr. Merrill was a big man, and, from a 4th grader's perspective, seemed like a giant. However, despite his size, he had a certain calmness about him. He seemed to glide when he walked. Things that would bother others rolled off him, as if his cheery mood couldn't be smudged by the trivial. There was an air of confidence that exuded from the authority of his voice, like that of a father. He liked being principal. He liked kids, and it showed. He smiled warmly at Matt. "Looks like you've been in quite a scrape. You want to tell me about it?"

Matt shrugged. "Not much to tell. I just got smashed playing Smear."

Mr. Merrill furrowed his brow. "Yes, that's what the nurse told me, but you and I know that isn't what really happened."

Matt looked away. "How did he know that? Maybe he's bluffing?" Matt looked back at Mr. Merrill. "I'm not sure what you mean?"

Mr. Merrill looked concerned. "It's OK, Matthew. I've already had a talk with TJ."

Matt smiled; he had watched enough television cop shows to know that Mr. Merrill was fishing. Besides, he'd been up against his mother's interrogation methods for years. "Oh I don't even remember TJ playing Smear, Sir. I'm pretty sure he wasn't one of the guys that tackled me."

Mr. Merrill chuckled. "OK, Tough Guy, you win. I'll find out what I want to know from some of TJ's friends. They're pretty easy to crack. Although you should think about what consequences might arise from lying to me about this."

Matt just looked at Mr. Merrill quietly. He knew that anything he said could incriminate him.

NEARFALL:

"Matthew, you see this scar on my forehead? I got this from being a tough guy that mixed it up with some older kids. I get to carry this scar as a reminder that handling big problems all on my own doesn't always work. Sometimes it's better to get some help. Now, I'm going to make this problem go away for you, but if you had come to me beforehand, you'd be a lot better looking right now."

Matt flashed his sure-fire grin. "I'll try to be more careful when I get tackled, Sir."

Mr. Merrill smiled. "Get back in class, you little scamp." Matt quickly ducked back into class. He didn't want to keep his "fans" waiting.

Jerry Rusk had been driving 18 wheelers for twenty five years, having crisscrossed the country more times than he could count. He'd seen his fair share of accidents and had a few close calls himself. However, as luck would have it, he'd never been the first person at the scene of accident. He was thankful for that. Life and death moments can be played out in the first minutes of a crash and that can be tough stuff to forget. He had trucker friends that were haunted by some of the grisly scenes they had witnessed at crash sites, and Jerry didn't want any part of it. Unfortunately, his circumstances were about to change.

He had just crested a small hill when he thought he saw what looked to be a car going over an embankment. It was quite a distance from him, perhaps as much as mile, so he couldn't be certain. He slowed his rig as he approached the spot where he guessed the car had gone off the road. Sure enough, there were car tracks in the dirt and it looked as though someone had hit the brakes.

Jerry pulled over to the shoulder and put his hazard lights on. His cheese-puff stained shirt bounced with his belly as he hopped

Chapter Nine

down from the cab and hustled to the edge of the road. There at the bottom of the hill was a car upside down with steam rising from the engine. Jerry sprinted back to the truck and got on the CB for help. He switched over to a police channel and called in the accident.

He ran back to the side of the road to look over the situation. The embankment dropped off at a steep angle, and Jerry was concerned that with his overweight condition, he might not be able to get down the hill without falling. "Ah, I should just wait until the professionals get here. What am I going to be able to do?" He thought about it a moment longer. "But I should check and see if there are people in there; I can at least tell them help is on the way." As Jerry debated his course of action, he thought he heard thumping coming from the car. He cocked his head to listen closely; there it was—a steady, constant pounding. "Ah, heck, someone is trying to get out."

Jerry stepped off the safety of the road and started down the hill. The grass was wet from rain the night before, and, as he feared, Jerry half fell, half walked down. He'd slide several feet, regain his footing, walk a couple steps, and end up on his side again, slipping his way down the slope. As he neared the car, he could see there was a man on the driver's side of the front seat. Jerry got within twenty feet of the car and came to an abrupt halt. "Whoa! That's gas, I'm not going any further." Jerry called out to Mr. Dean in the front seat, "Hey Buddy, there's help on the way. Just hang in there." Mr. Dean, half conscious and still kicking, didn't hear him. Jerry looked around; the seconds were ticking off like a bomb. "Come on. Where are those state patrol guys?" Jerry listened for sirens. More seconds passed and there was no sound except the constant thumping coming from inside the car. "Ah heck! The Lord hates a coward."

Mrs. Dean had been humming to herself ever since the phone

call from her husband. It was such a relief to know that he'd gotten the job. She didn't like that he would have a long commute, but it was an increase in pay over his previous job. Maybe now they could start that college fund for the boys that they always talked about. Mrs. Dean, as usual, was a whirl of activity. She'd already cleaned up the house, completed two loads of laundry (with a third in process), gotten the mail, weeded the garden and fed the cat.

Now she was on to food prep—she intended to surprise her husband with a feast for dinner. She pulled several thick steaks from the deep freeze. They had been held in reserve for just such a celebratory meal. On her way back to the kitchen she grabbed the potatoes and canned green beans from the pantry. Just as her arms were laden with food, the phone rang. "Naturally," she muttered to herself. She tried to rearrange the things she was carrying, but gave up as the phone rang for the third time. "I'm coming," she yelled out to the phone as if the person on the other end could hear her. She half jogged down the hall, dropping a can of beans in the process. "Hello," she blurted as she tucked the phone between her ear and shoulder. "Yes, this is Mrs. Dean." Her face blanched white and the food tumbled to the floor. "Yes, of course, I'll be there right away."

Dan met Mike in the hall after class, and they headed for their lockers.

"So what did you get on that test?" Dan asked.

"I got an A-," Mike guiltily responded.

"Awww man, you're a jerk. I got a D. Well, at least I passed, so the old man won't get his underwear in a bunch. So what did ol' four eyes get?" Dan was, of course, referring to Billy and his coke bottle glasses.

Chapter Nine

"He got a B+. I think that's part of the reason he was so ticked off."

Dan laughed, "Gee, ya think?" Dan cringed, holding his head; he was still feeling the impact of his behavior from the previous day.

Mike looked at his buddy. "So thanks for bailing me out with the little spider dance. I'm sure it hurt."

"No problem. I'll probably pee blood for a week, but what are friends for." Mike laughed at Dan's dramatic flair.

"So what's Billy going to hold you to? What do you have to do for him?"

"I'm not sure," Mike responded.

"Well, just make sure that it doesn't require you dressing up like Princess Leia."

Mike laughed loudly, and Dan shushed him, "Come on Dude, not so loud." Dan looked up to see the school police liaison standing near their lockers. "Mike, look."

Mike's smile quickly faded. He glanced at Dan. "Do you think you're busted?"

Dan was in a total panic internally but had the presence of mind to tell Mike, "Be cool."

As the boys took the last few steps toward their lockers, Officer Tuttle addressed them. You're Michael Dean, right?"

Mike was shocked to have the question directed to him; Dan looked equally puzzled. Mike, in his bewilderment, stumbled over his answer, "Uh, who me? Umm, yeah, I'm Michael Dean."

"Mike, I'm Officer Tuttle. I'm sorry to tell you this, but your father has been in a serious car accident, and I've been instructed to take you up to the hospital."

Matt was busy writing out a response to Kim's note that had been slipped to him. Despite the "danger," or perhaps because of it, Kimberly was hoping to have lunch with Matt today. Matt couldn't have been more thrilled; Mr. Merrill was closing in on TJ, and TJ wouldn't dare risk doing anything further to Matt until things calmed down. Matt felt complete satisfaction. "Love" had triumphed. He had taken TJ's best shot and still won the girl. Life was good.

At that moment, there was a small knock on the door and Mr. Merrill stepped into the room. "Mrs. Wilson, I apologize for interrupting, but I'm going to need to see Matthew again, please." Matt got up from his chair and smiled at Kimberly. As he walked to the door, he thought, "That was fast. TJ's buddies must have gone Benedict Arnold on him in a hurry."

Mr. Merrill put his hand on the back of Matt's shoulder guiding him into the hall and closed the door behind them. His normal cheery demeanor was replaced by a deeply saddened expression. "Matt, your grandparents are coming to pick you up."

Matt was mystified. Was he being suspended? Mr. Merrill continued, "I don't want to worry you or scare you, but your Dad's in the hospital. He was in a car accident. Your brother and your Mom are going to meet you at the hospital."

Matt immediately felt like the wind had been knocked out of him, and his eyes filled with tears. All of sudden he didn't feel like a "tough guy."

Chapter Nine

Mike waited at the nurse's station as he was instructed by the police liaison. His mind swirled with questions as his stomach did flip flops. "Where are Mom and Matt? Why won't they let me see Dad? How did this happen?" The emotions were flooding in. It was overwhelming, and, just as he felt like he might lose it, he heard his name, "Michael." It was his grandma and grandpa, and they had Matt in tow. Grandma wrapped her arms around Mike. "It's going to be all right. Your father is in surgery right now, and the doctors are going to get him fixed up."

Mike knew, of course, that she probably didn't know any more than he did, but it didn't matter. He felt much better just to have her comfort. Grandpa put a hand on his shoulder, "Don't worry Son. Your dad is as tough as nails. He'll be OK."

Mike looked at Matthew and pulled himself together. He was the big brother, and he didn't want Matt to get more worried just because he couldn't keep his emotions in check. "Where's Mom?" Mike asked.

"She's talking to one of the doctors and taking care of all the paperwork. She's going to meet us in the waiting room when she's done. Why don't you two boys take a seat while your grandfather and I talk to this nice man that drove you from the school."

Matt and Mike dutifully sat down while their grandparents spoke with the officer. Mike glanced over at Matt—he was very quiet, looking down at his shoes and virtually motionless. This was a radical departure for Matt; normally he'd be fidgeting in his seat like he had ants in his pants. Matthew, perhaps sensing his brother's gaze, asked the question that was in the pit of his stomach. "Is Dad going to die?"

This caught Mike completely off guard, and he defensively reacted, "What!? No, he's not going to die. You heard Grandpa. Dad is as tough as nails. He's just a little banged up."

Matt had more. "Tony LeMay's dad was a body builder, and he was killed in a car wreck."

Mike countered, "Yeah, but Mr. LeMay got hit by a semi-truck. I don't think Dad got hit by anything." Mike hoped that would calm Matt, but, in truth, Matt had a pretty good point—people sometimes die in car wrecks.

"OK, Boys, let's head over to the waiting room and get some sodas. How about that?"

The boys just sat there. The tension of Matt's question still hung in the air. Grandpa was a former train engineer for the Burlington Northern railroad and was missing the middle finger on his right hand from a rail yard accident. He liked to joke that he gave people the finger all the time, but no one understood why he was shaking a fist at them. At the moment, he was just trying to distract his grandsons.

"All right, if that's the way you're going to be, here's the way I feel about it." He shook his fist with the amputated finger at them, and mocked being offended.

Matt smiled slightly at his grandfather's antics, and Grandpa again prodded them, "Come on, guys. I know it's rough, but let's go get those sodas—maybe we can rustle up something to eat, too. You guys are probably getting hungry." Mike and Matt slid out of their chairs and shuffled off in the direction of the "family lounge." Grandma had finished up with the officer and led them down the hall.

Mrs. Dean waited quietly. She needed to get all the paperwork filled out so that her husband could be officially admitted to the hospital. When the people in front of her finally finished, she approached the desk and took a seat.

"I'm here for my husband, Peter Dean. He was brought in by ambulance from a car accident."

"Oh, I'm so sorry Ma'am, I didn't realize you were waiting to see me. I apologize; I could have gotten you started on this paperwork. I'll let the nurse's station know that you are here with me."

Mrs. Dean's hands were shaking as she answered the questions on the medical history forms. She looked up, slightly embarrassed—usually she kept a level head in a crisis. "Goodness, I don't know why I'm shaking so, this certainly isn't the first time I've been in an emergency room. I've got two boys, and they've had their share of stitches and other mishaps."

The admitting attendant was a heavyset woman with a kind face and a hint of an Irish accent. "It's all right Ma'am. Take your time. It's perfectly natural to be a little shook up. Just know that these doctors deal with this kind of thing all the time. Your husband is in good hands." Mrs. Dean smiled meekly. "Do you have your insurance card, Ma'am?"

Mrs. Dean flinched. In an instant the realization hit her, "Oh, my God. How are we going to pay for this?" With Mr. Dean out of work they hadn't had enough money to get primary insurance. She dug through her purse. "Yes, I have it here somewhere." She pulled out their card, knowing that it was just a supplemental insurance and would probably not cover very much.

"OK, I'll just need to make a copy of this and put it with your file."

The panic was rising in Mrs. Dean's throat. All she could think of at the moment was her husband. "What if he needs a procedure, and they won't give it to him because he doesn't have enough coverage? What am I going to do?" She took a deep breath. "OK. First things first, he's alive, and that's the most important thing. Just take it one step at a time." She was coaching herself through, and it was working. She was regaining composure.

From around the corner, a nurse approached. "Mrs. Dean, your husband is out of surgery, and we're putting him in a recovery room. Would you like to come with me to see the doctor?"

Matt looked around the room. They had been waiting for what seemed like hours. There were a couple of other families waiting for loved ones or waiting to hear how someone was doing. Everybody, it seemed, was talking in that hushed tone people use when they're really worried. Grandpa was periodically regaling Matt and Mike with stories about their father, reassuring them about how smart he was and how tough he was. The stories all started pretty much the same, "There was this one time…" but most importantly it was working. and Matt was starting to feel a little better. He took a big bite of the submarine sandwich that Grandma had gotten for him at the hospital cafeteria. Mike, of course, had already finished his and was pumping money into the vending machine for a snack. It seemed that he was always hungry.

"That's good. Eat up. I don't want your dad upset with me, because I didn't get you enough food."

Matt couldn't really imagine his dad getting mad at Grandpa, but it was nice to think that his dad would be awake and talking yet tonight. Matt glanced up at the TV. It was a reporter talking on the side of highway, the sound was down, but Matt could see it was the site of a crash.

In the background a mangled shell of a car was being loaded onto the flatbed of a truck. The camera zoomed in on the car as it was lowered. Matt's eyes widened and with a mouthful of food, he pointed at the television. "Look! It's Dad's car."

They each turned their attention to the images on the screen. It was Mr. Dean's car, and not only was it crushed; it was burned to a crisp. Whatever good feelings Grandpa had been able to generate quickly disappeared; the car was completely totaled. Matt looked at his brother who was now staring at the television with his mouth open.

Grandpa tried to recover, but he couldn't look Matt in the face as he trotted out the line, "It just looks worse than it is." Matt's grandma became instantly upset and excused herself from the room. Matt could feel his body tighten as the fear grabbed hold, "I just want to see my dad."

The nurse led Mrs. Dean down the corridor...

CHAPTER 10

Dr. Walter Roberts was a gentle man. He spoke softly and carefully, for he wanted to both comfort and educate Mrs. Dean on her husband's condition.

"Mrs. Dean, your husband did very well in surgery and is stable; he's being moved from the recovery room to the intensive care unit."

"Can I see him?" Mrs. Dean asked.

The doctor nodded, "Yes. However, he'll be groggy from the surgery, and we have him sedated. Right now we have a tube down his throat to help him breathe."

Mrs. Dean covered her mouth in fear and the doctor continued. "Now, don't worry. This is normal considering the nature of the injuries your husband sustained. He has a collapsed lung and a couple of broken ribs, so we needed to assist him with his breathing. We inserted a chest tube so that we can gradually re-inflate his lung. Your husband also has a compound facture of his thigh-

Chapter Ten

bone, and his pelvis was cracked. We've been able to repair the break by realigning the bone and inserting a metal plate secured with screws to help bolster the strength of the area that was damaged. The fracture in the pelvis was minimal and doesn't appear to be load bearing, so that should heal on its own with some time. That being said, he will need significant bed rest."

Mrs. Dean listened carefully, but the worry that filled her heart could no longer be contained. "Is he going to be OK?" she asked.

The doctor chose his sentences guardedly. "I would expect him to recover nicely. Still, I must caution these are serious injuries and we're not completely out of the woods yet. There is a fairly large blood loss associated with this type of trauma. One of our concerns is what happens when the blood clots. It can be life threatening if a clot breaks loose and gets in the lungs, so we need to keep his leg elevated and keep compression on the lower part of his legs. Infection is also a real risk, so we'll be monitoring him very closely for the next couple of days. On the positive side, he doesn't seem to have any head injuries or additional internal bleeding and was responsive and talking when they brought him into emergency."

Mrs. Dean hadn't heard that her husband was conscious upon arriving at the hospital. "He was talking? What was he saying?"

The Dr. Roberts smiled. "He was asking if we could cast his leg quickly so that he could make it to work tomorrow."

Mrs. Dean smiled. "Well, that sounds like him. Thank you very much, Doctor."

Mr. Dean attempted to open his eyes, but each eyelid felt like it weighed a hundred pounds. He could hear sounds around him—the beeping of monitors, the low hum of electric motors, and in the distance he could hear voices talking—it sounded like it might be a nurse's station. He commanded his eyes to open; he could only pry them open for a moment. It was apparent that he was in a hospital room, but in the little glimpse his eyelids allowed, he couldn't determine how badly he was dinged up. He remembered the accident and being loaded in the ambulance, but things were a bit foggy after that.

As Mr. Dean tried to recall what was said in the emergency room, the sensation of the room spinning hit him. "Ugh," he thought. His stomach began to whirl and he felt as though he might vomit. He tried to swallow, but couldn't. His throat was obstructed, "Oh brother, I've got a tube down my throat. How bad off am I? I need to get out of here."

As he panicked, he attempted to move, but stabbing pain engulfed the side of this chest, and his leg felt as though it might disconnect from his body. Mr. Dean let his head fall back into the pillow. "This might take a while. What am I going to tell my wife?"

Mike and Matt sat quietly with their grandparents. Gone were the attempts by Grandpa to keep their spirits up. Grandma was having a difficult time keeping her composure, although, for her grandchildren's sake, she brushed her tears off, and half-heartedly smiled, saying, "Old ladies can get overly emotional."

The pictures of Mr. Dean's car on the newscast really had everyone shaken up. Mike, who had emphatically rejected the question by his younger brother of whether their dad might die, was now locked into his own mental battle between trying to think positively and being scared beyond belief. Grandpa looked over his grandsons. He was proud of them; they were doing their best to hang tough.

"What happened to your face, Matthew?"

Chapter Ten

Matt started to reach for the 'getting tackled in Smear' answer, but instead told the truth. "I like this girl at school named Kimberly, and there's this guy named TJ that's older than me, well he likes her too. So he beat me up. I even lost a tooth, but I didn't cry, and Kimberly likes me even more now." Matt was matter of fact in his delivery of the story, as if he were reading a menu.

His grandpa didn't know quite how to react. "Well, that's good...I guess."

Matt's grandma, who seemed lost in her own thoughts, snapped back to reality. "Did you just say some boy beat you up? Who was this? What started the fight? Has your mother called the school? Oh my goodness! Look at your face. You're all bruised up."

Grandpa put his hand on his wife's forearm to reassure her. "Just let it go, Dear."

Matt couldn't believe they hadn't noticed his face up to this point. They had picked him up from school, and he rode to the hospital with them. In any case, the fight with TJ seemed unimportant at the moment.

He looked at his brother. "A lot has happened the last couple days, huh?"

Mike nodded yes and posed his own question, "Someone should be able to tell us what's going on with Dad. I wonder where Mom is?"

Grandma spoke up again, "Boys, maybe we should say a prayer for your father."

Mrs. Dean braced for what she might see as she entered the room. She gasped as she saw her husband lying in the bed. He looked so helpless. There were cords everywhere, blood was going into his arm, his leg was up in the air, and there was a little bubbler of some sort on the side of the bed, along with several monitors. His chin was bandaged, he was bruised on his arms and forehead. It looked every bit as serious as the doctor made it sound.

She rolled a chair up to his bed and sat down. She looked at his hand and remembered a hot shot guy with a devilish grin giving her a hard time while she tried to take his order. She remembered the jolt she felt when he grabbed her hand on the way out of the restaurant and asked for her phone number. The palm of the hand in front of her now in the hospital was where she wrote her number. She smiled at the memory and put her hand on his. "Peter, can you hear me, Hon? It's me."

Mr. Dean had gradually been gaining more functions as the minutes went by. He opened his eyes, and turned his head very slightly to look at his wife. He could see that she had been crying. It killed him to know that he was causing so much worry. He wanted to reassure her, so he gave her a little wink.

She stood up and gave him a kiss on the forehead. "Oh you still think you're charming even in this condition, huh?"

He gave her a feeble "thumbs up" in response.

She laughed. "Well, I guess you'll live then. I love you so much, you big jerk. You scared me half to death. How many times have I told you to keep both hands on the wheel?" Mr. Dean rolled his eyes. "The doc says you're going to be just fine. You've got a broken leg and you cracked a couple ribs. Are you doing all right?"

Mr. Dean made the "OK" sign with his finger and thumb.

"The boys are here; do you want to see them?"

Chapter Ten

Mr. Dean gingerly shook his head, "No."

"Are you sure? Because they would like to see you."

Again Mr. Dean meekly shook his head "No."

"You just don't want them to see you like this?"

He gave a "thumbs up" in response.

"Well, maybe you're right. They might get scared to see you this ugly, although in general, most mornings you look pretty frightening, so really this isn't that bad." Mr. Dean's raised his eyebrows in response to his wife's gallows humor. "Your parents are here, too. Do you want to let them come see you?"

Mr. Dean with great difficulty nodded yes. Of course he wanted to see his boys more than anything in the world, but he didn't want them to be scared. Maybe tomorrow he'd have the tube out and could talk to them. He knew his parents were more likely to handle the situation.

"Well, OK, Hon. I'm going to go talk to the boys. They haven't had anything explained to them yet, and I'm sure they are plenty upset. I'll come back with your parents. OK?"

Mr. Dean again gave a weak "OK" sign.

"You stay here and get better. Try to heal fast. I love you, my darling man."

Mr. Dean reached up and grabbed her hand. He gave it a gentle squeeze.

"Hey, you know this isn't that bad. At least I can always get the last word in." She kissed him on the forehead again, walked across the room and closed the door behind her. She rounded the corner in the hallway, fell against the wall and burst out into tears. She held it together for as long as she could for her husband's sake, but, in truth, she was scared to death. This family was her life, and it just didn't work without him. He had to be OK.

She quickly recovered her poise. She was a jumbled bundle of raw nerves, but she needed to pull it together for her family—especially for her boys. She admonished herself, almost to the point of being angry, "Now, get it together. You can't fall apart here. You don't have that option." She wiped away her tears, straightened her blouse, pulled back her shoulders, and headed for the waiting room. She needed to be calm and cheerful by the time they saw her. There was no sense in needlessly worrying them.

Mike was becoming increasingly agitated. "Someone ought to have come and told us something by now." Grandpa, who had been deftly deflecting these statements for quite a while, finally broke. "Yeah, I tend to agree with you. I think we should have heard something by now too."

He looked out into the hall to see if he might be able to collar a nurse. Instead he noticed Mike's mom trying to get his attention. They made eye contact and she pointed that she was going to duck down another corridor. Mike was looking out the window, and Matt was reading a magazine, so neither one of them noticed their mother in the hallway.

Grandpa stood up and announced that he was going to see if he could find some information. "I'll be right back." He walked out into the hallway and turned the corner where his daughter-in-law was "hiding."

Mrs. Dean smiled and gave Grandpa a hug. "Sorry for the cloak and dagger, but I didn't want the boys to see me."

Grandpa looked puzzled. "What's going on? Is Peter OK?"
Mrs. Dean nodded. "Yes, I just came from his room. He's doing fine, but he didn't want the boys to see him right now — he's got a breathing tube ventilator thing, and he can't talk right now. He's conscious, and the doctor said the only real risk at this point is clotting and infection, but other than that he's going to be OK."

Grandpa gave out a huge sigh and put his hands on his knees before straightening back up with a big grin on his face. "Oh that's great. Whew, I feel like I can breathe again."

Mrs. Dean, concerned that she may have painted too rosy a picture, tried to tamp down the expectations. "He's still in intensive care, and they'll need to keep a close eye on him, because I guess he lost quite a lot of blood. They also have him sedated, so he's not that chipper."

Grandpa was still smiling. "That's fine. That's fine, just as long as I know he's whole and OK. Can we see him?"

"Yes, he'd like to see you. He's on the third floor, bed five. I'll explain things to the kids, and you can make some excuse about going to the cafeteria for a cup of coffee."

Grandpa nodded, "OK. That sounds good."

They walked into the waiting room together, and Grandpa announced, "Look who I found wandering the hallways."

The boys in unison practically shrieked, "Mom!" They ran and gave her a big hug. Matt blurted out, "Is Dad all burned up? Is he going to die?"

NEARFALL:

Mrs. Dean looked at him bewildered. "Burned? Whatever gave you that idea?"

"On the news they showed Dad's car and it was burnt like a french-fry."

Mrs. Dean seemed somewhat taken aback by this revelation. "Well, I can assure your Dad is not burned. I just spoke to him."

Mike was cautious, "So he's going to be OK?"

"Yes, Michael, he's going to be fine. He broke his leg, and he's got some other bumps and bruises, but he's going to be all right."

Grandpa turned to his bride. "Come on Margaret. Let's go get a cup of coffee."

"But I don't want coffee."

Grandpa sighed, "How about some tea then?"

Grandpa made a motion toward the door with his head, and Grandma finally got the hint, although she didn't seem to be pleased about leaving. "Oh, all right, perhaps some tea will be nice. I might as well keep the old goat company."

Mrs. Dean sat down, and the boys peppered her with questions. "So can we go see him?"

"Well, your father is sleeping now and is very tired from the surgery, so I think it would be better if we wait until tomorrow."

Matt weighed in with his next question, "Does he have any stitches?"

Mrs. Dean paused to think. "You know, I'm not sure. I think he had some on his chin, but it was under a bandage, so I couldn't say for sure. And I'm guessing he probably has some stitches in his leg where they did the surgery."

Mike asked, "Does he know that we're here?"

"Yes, he knows very well that you are here and he said he loves you both very much. He was sorry that you had to miss class on his account."

Mike smiled. That sounded like his father. He didn't want anyone missing any school work.

"So, are we going to school tomorrow?" Matt wanted to know.

"Well, I think we can discuss that at dinner."

Mike asked, "How did the accident happen?"

"You know what? I didn't ask your dad that question. I know the police officer said that he went off the side of the road and into a little ravine."

Matt excitedly described what was on the news. "Yeah, they showed it on TV. It was really steep and Dad's car was completely smashed. It must have rolled like twenty times!"

Mrs. Dean cringed at the description. "That's enough. I don't want to hear anymore."

"Aww Mom. It's all right. Dad's OK, but we're going to need a new car. You know what's cool—the new Mustang. Can we get one of those Mom? Can we please?"

"Matthew, I have no earthly idea what kind of car we're going to get, but, unless Mustang makes a station wagon, I doubt we'll be getting one."

"Aww man!" Matt sat back in his chair with his arms across his chest. Mike was still trying to sort things out. He knew his Mom well enough to know that she'd put a positive spin on things. "So what part of the leg did he break?"

"He broke the bone in his thigh, and they put it back together and put a little metal plate in there to make sure it heals strong. That's what took so long, that and all the paperwork that I had to fill out."

Mike seemed satisfied with the answer. "So when do we eat?"

"Well, I'm going to go check on your grandparents and determine what they want to do. I'm also going to stop by the nurse's station and see if there is anything else that I have to do before we can leave. You boys stay here, and I'll be back in a few minutes."

Mrs. Dean felt that it had gone reasonably well with her sons; all in all, they seemed to be handling everything thrown at them. She could see the worry in their faces, but they were holding it together. She bit the side of her bottom lip. It was a nervous habit. She was anxious to get back to her husband's room and see him again before she took the kids home for the day. However, she also wanted to get out of the hospital before someone could easily corner her about their medical coverage. "Tomorrow I'll have to sit down with the hospital and see if we can work out some sort of payment plan. Maybe tonight I'll purchase a lotto ticket."

CHAPTER 11

Billy Johnson had been annoyed the entire day, and now, on his short walk home, he was still mumbling to himself, "I should have turned him in right then and there. Why did I let him off the hook? It would have been so great to seem him humiliated in front of the entire class. Mr. Rhenkin would have flunked him for sure, and all would be right in the universe; another jock bites the dust." Billy clenched his fists in frustration. "Why didn't I just turn him in?"

Billy had endured his fair share of ridicule from the "in" crowd, and he viewed Mike to be firmly entrenched in the lemming realm of stupid and muscle-bound. However, he did make a mental note that Mike was one of the few people who actually took interest in what Billy was reading and, in fact, asked a couple decent questions about mythology—the topic so near and dear to Billy's heart. Maybe that's why in the midst of Mike's pleading for leniency, Billy wavered. "No matter, he's still a jock and deserves whatever I can come up with for a penalty."

As he covered the last couple of blocks to his house, Billy tried to come up with a suitable consequence, but he was drawing blanks. There were only so many things he could force Mike to do without possibly getting in trouble himself. For instance, if he forced Mike to run down the hall with his pants on his head, Mike was sure to crack and tell who put him up to it. Besides, in his "cool" anti-establishment bizarre world, such a moron thing to do would probably only serve to make Mike more likable—he'd be the rebel without a clue. As Billy walked up the front steps of his house, he assured himself that he'd come up with something.

He dropped his book bag in the entryway, grabbed a cookie from the kitchen, and plodded upstairs to his room. As he reached the top of the stairs and turned to go down the hallway, he heard sobbing from his sister Kimberly's room. The door was slightly ajar, and he pushed it open. The overwhelming pink that enveloped his sister's room was still shocking, even though he had seen it countless times before.

"What's wrong with you?"

"Nothing. Leave me alone, Billy. Just go watch Star Trek or something."

Billy was concerned; his sister wasn't one to cry. "Is there something wrong with Mom?"

Kimberly looked up. "No."

Billy pressed more, "Well, what is it then?"

Kimberly wiped her eyes. "It's nothing, it's stupid. I don't even know why I'm crying."

Billy continued to stand in the doorway. He and his sister might be complete opposites, but she was still his baby sister. Seeing that her brother was worried and not leaving, she blurted out, "I like this boy in my class and his dad was in car crash today and they came to get him out of school to go up to the hospital. And I'm just worried about him. That's all. I'm sure he's sad and scared."

Billy wasn't sure how to respond. "What's his name?"

Kimberly sniffled and said, "Matthew Dean."

Billy's eyes squinted in dismay. "Dean? His last name is Dean? He wouldn't happen to have an older brother would he?"

Kimberly nodded. "Actually, I think he goes to your school."

Billy spouted off from the hip, "Well, that guy is a jerk, which means his brother is probably a jerk too. You should stay away from that family."

Kimberly looked at her brother in amazement. "I tell you that the boy I like has a father lying in the hospital, and all you can say is that his brother is a jerk? I don't understand how I ended up with such a dork for an older brother."

Billy reacted in a fashion typical of the many fights he had with his sister. "Yeah, well why don't you go play with your Barbie and Ken dolls and make up stories for your pretty little world with your pea-sized, pretty little brain."

"Just leave me alone, Billy!"

He slammed the door to her room. "Fine!"

He trudged off to his room and laid on his bed--staring at the ceiling with his hands behind his head. His thoughts drifted back to

NEARFALL:

Mike Dean. "Maybe I should just let it go; having your dad in the hospital is punishment enough." Billy was sensitive on this topic having had his own father die of a heart attack when he was only eight. Possibly his sister was reliving some of the feelings from their own father's death. He hadn't thought of that. As he got up to go apologize to his sister he thought, "How do I back this up? She's not going to listen to me."

Billy slowly walked down the hall. Deep down he knew his sister was right. He was a dork, and, although she was only in fourth grade, she was definitely the type that taunted him. She was pretty, smart, fit, and knew every song on the radio. In truth, he was proud of his sister, although he worried about her becoming one of "them"—more accurately he worried that she wouldn't like him as she got older. He felt it was already starting to happen.

He could still remember when she would run and jump on him with reckless abandon, pleading with him to give her a horsey-back ride. She wasn't aware of the world then. He was just her big brother. But as he reached her door, he knew she wasn't just acting out. She really felt those words, "I don't understand how I ended up with such a dork for a brother."

Oh, how he wished he could turn back the clock to a time when it didn't matter. "Why does it matter to anyone?" He had built a wall around himself from the teasing he received at school, but occasionally he was still hurt by it. He told himself countless times, "Sticks and stones can break your bones, but words can never hurt you." Despite keeping his guard up, he had to acknowledge that sometimes the words do hurt—especially when they come from someone you love.

He was like any kid. He wanted to be accepted, he wanted to have friends—he just didn't know how to break through—how to connect. "Maybe that's my punishment for Mike; he has to help me be cool."

He opened the door. "Billy, please just let me be. I don't want to fight with you."

"OK, I don't want to fight with you, either. Hey, Kim, do you ever think about Dad?"

Kimberly who had been lying face first on the bed, turned over on her side to look at her brother. "I can hardly remember him. It's like he's fading away. I try, but I just can't see him clearly anymore."

Kimberly's voice cracked with emotion. Billy wanted to go to her, but he stood planted in the doorway. "I can help you remember. Do you remember when he would make buckwheat pancakes on Saturday mornings? He'd always be wearing his slippers and that blue bath robe. We'd complain that it was buckwheat, and he would say it puts hair on your chest. Or the time when he took us out in the garden to show us how to plant corn? You had a big hat with a daisy on the front and matching boots. Dad always called you his little Kimmers or Kimberly Boo, remember? He would have you take his shoes off, and every time you'd tell him how stinky his feet were. Sometimes he would burp at the table, and Mom would get mad at him, and, when she wasn't looking, he would wink at us. He always cut the turkey at Thanksgiving and made a big deal out of it, and every Christmas he would lift you up so that you could put the star on the Christmas tree. He had those big arms, and that big belly... I remember you would poke him in the stomach and he would squeal like the Pillsbury dough-boy, and we would all laugh. He had such a big laugh. It seemed like it would shake the whole room.

Billy's voice trailed off—the memories became so thick they

NEARFALL:

gathered as mist in Kimberly's eyes, rolled down her cheeks, and had to be wiped away.

He looked at his sister. "Dad loved you more than anything, and I know he's watching out for you now."

Kimberly got up from her bed, crossed the room, and threw her arms around her big brother. "Thank you, I do remember those things. I'm sorry for what I said earlier."

"I'm sorry too, Kimberly Boo."

Dan looked at the clock in the hallway; he had stalled as long as he could, but if he didn't get going now he was going to be late to practice—and no way could he handle extra laps. He grabbed his jacket from his locker and then shuffled off toward the gym.

He was absolutely dreading this practice. Not only was he hung over, but he was worried about Mr. Dean, and it weighed on him heavily. He really just wanted to bug out and head over to the hospital.

As his teammates were getting changed for practice Dan made sure the coach was aware of why Mike was absent from practice. Of course he also needed to explain his own absence from the day before. The fact that Dan was still "sick" made his excuse for missing practice somewhat believable. Once practice started any skepticism his coach had of his story quickly disappeared. To say that Dan's performance left much to be desired was like saying the Pacific Ocean was a small pool of water.

He was winded and sweating profusely during warm-ups. While drilling technique he was as graceful as an NFL lineman in the ballet. It was brutal, ugly, and tough to watch. When the practice moved on to live wrestling, Dan struggled to tie his opponents up and hang on for dear life. Usually the best on the team, Dan found himself getting thrashed by guys that he would normally pin. If nothing else, he certainly helped build the confidence of some of his teammates.

His shots were so pathetic that at one point, his coach suggested that he sit out the rest of practice. Dan would have loved to have taken him up on the offer, but he knew that it had been Mr. Dean's intention to call the coach and make today's practice especially difficult. Dan thought he owed it to Mr. Dean to suffer. During conditioning, Dan was dead last and focused mostly on trying not to pass out. When practice mercifully came to an end, Dan found an empty quiet spot on the floor and laid there for 20 minutes with a towel over his head just trying to gather his strength for a shower. "Just shoot me if I ever drink again. This sucks."

His coach walked through the room and spied Dan's carcass. "Are you going up to the hospital?" Coach McCreary asked. Dan looked out from underneath the towel. "Yeah, as soon as I get home." Coach tapped his foot into Dan's rib cage. "Well, get a move on, you need to get showered up." Dan rolled over and worked his way to his feet. Coach turned as he was walking away. "Make sure you give the Dean family my best, and tell Mike to take all the time he needs." "Will do, Coach, will do."

Dan knew he needed to make an appearance at home before he could go to the hospital. It had been three days since he was last at home, and his father was sure to notice his absence. Usually, if Dan was gone for a day, it passed without incident. His dad worked in construction, putting in a lot of overtime hours and when he wasn't busy with work, he was, as a rule, drinking heavily.

Dan could usually fly below the radar. He could even stay at the Dean's most nights, but he had to stop at his house almost daily. Three days was pushing the envelope, if for no other reason than his dad would see that no one had cleaned up. The key for Dan was to make sure he did the jobs he was assigned and then just stay out of the way. Dan knew, if he could empty the garbage, do his dad's dishes, clean the kitchen, and pick up all the beer cans scattered around the house—he might be able to slip back out and jog over to the hospital. It really depended on how far into the case of beer his dad had gotten. It was a difficult balancing act. If his father was completely sober, he'd rattle off a bunch of chores and make Dan do his homework. If he was early into the drinking, he'd be agreeable and fairly mellow, even chatty. The worst scenario was if Dan caught his father as he started to get plastered, somewhere between half and three quarters of a case. At that point, he could be mean, loud, and abusive.

Dan had long since invented all sorts of ways to "disappear." The best was to offer to run to the gas station and pick up some more cigarettes. His old man would give him the cash, and Dan would make sure he didn't come home until his dad was passed out. The easiest state of affairs was when his father was on his last few beers. By then he just sat in front of the television in a semi-comatose stupor. Dan could get the household tasks done and leave without his dad noticing or remembering.

Despite the easy option, Dan usually tried to time it for the beginning of the case of beer. There was more risk in this, but he liked the occasional moments when his father seemed "normal." He didn't even mind being forced to do homework. As Dan walked up to the house, he peeked in the window. His father was sitting in his usual chair in front of the television, with a cigarette in one hand and a beer in the other. Dan looked at the clock in the living room; it was almost 6:30.

On most nights it would still be the near the beginning phase of drinking—depending on when his father got off from work. Dan winced when he peered through the glass in the direction of the kitchen. The sink was overflowing with dishes, and the garbage can had spilled over onto the floor. The safe play was to wait for a couple hours before going in, but then it would be too late for visiting hours at the hospital.

Dan steeled himself and decided to go in. "Well, it's probably still early; if I'm lucky, he should be in a good mood." Dan pulled open the outer metal door with its torn screen and cracked window. He pushed open the interior wooden door that led into the living room. As he stepped into the house he was greeted with an empty beer can whizzing past his head, hitting the door frame behind him. "Where the hell you been?" barked his father. Dan knew instantly—being lucky was not going to be in the cards.

CHAPTER 12

Dan had been knocked around by his dad before, so it was no big deal. At worst, he was going to have a shiner tomorrow. All he needed to do was finish with the dishes and then he could dash to the hospital. Dan picked up the frying pan filled with pork chop grease and dumped it into the trash. He wiped down the stove. "What a slob. Doesn't he eat anything other than burnt meat?" Dan thought about it. Other than Thanksgiving or a meal someone else had cooked, he didn't think he'd ever seen his father eat a vegetable that wasn't a potato. Dan was cruising at light speed trying to finish everything up. He wiped down the kitchen counter and threw the dishrag in the dirty laundry. He walked toward his dad's room, glancing at his father as he ambled past him in the living room. He was still awake, unfortunately.

Mike hustled to his father's nightstand and grabbed the phone and phone book. He got the number for the hospital and dialed. He knew his father wouldn't hear anything over the noise of the television.

"Memorial Hospital, how can I help you?"

Chapter Twelve

Dan lowered his voice, "Ah yes, I was wondering if you could give me Peter Dean's room please."

"I'll transfer you Sir."

Elevator music came on while he was waiting. He couldn't be certain, but he was pretty sure it was an instrumental version of the Beatles song "Help" which seemed rather amusing for a hospital.

"Sir, Mr. Dean is in intensive care and can't receive phone calls. Are you family?"

"Yes, I'm his brother." Dan crossed his fingers hoping his bluff would work.

"Well, Sir I can give you the direct number for the intensive care nurses station. However, visiting hours are over, and you'll need to call back tomorrow."

Dan covered the phone, not knowing what to do. He finally jumped back on. "Umm, that will be fine; however I'll be in town in the morning and I'll just stop by the hospital. Could you tell me what room he's in?"

"Yes Sir. He's in intensive care bed five."

Dan scribbled it down on a piece of paper, "Thank you so much."

"You have a great evening, Sir."

Dan hung up and quickly dialed the Dean house, but the phone rang off the hook—no answer. Dan slammed the phone down in frustration and then cringed when he realized it was excessively loud and extremely stupid. He tip-toed to the door and looked out through the crack in the door jam. His father apparently hadn't heard anything, because the only reaction from him appeared to be excessive scratching of his belly and nether regions. Dan recoiled, "That's disgusting." He paced the room and tried the Deans again—no luck. "I've got to find out what's going on. I'll just go the hospital and see if I can charm a nurse or something."

Dan grabbed the beer cans from under the bed and headed back out into the living room. He dumped them into the garbage, tied up the bag, grabbed his jacket, and started to head for the door.

"Where the hell do you think you're going?" Dan's father struggled to his feet.

"Um, well I was just going up to the hospital and check on Mike's dad."

"He's not your dad. I'm your dad, so what the hell difference does it make?"

Dan could tell that his father would pass out soon. He just needed to weather the storm in the meantime. "Yeah, I know you're my dad. I was just going up there for moral support."

"Aw, bull! Moral support? You don't think I know you like him better than me?"

"Dad, that's crazy. Come on. Let me help you sit back down."

Dan tried to guide him back to the chair, but his father cuffed him in the head. "Don't paw me, Boy. Just keep your hands off me. I sit down when I feel like sitting down. You hear me? Huh? You hear me?"

He slapped Dan in the face. "Yeah, I hear ya, Dad. I tell you what. I won't go. I'll just take the trash out like you asked, and then I'll

Chapter Twelve

run to the gas station and get you some more cigarettes, OK?"

"I don't need any more cigs. You're not going anywhere." Dan tried to keep him talking; it was fairly easy to manipulate him when he was this drunk. He was slurring his words and swaying on his feet.

"OK. Well, if you don't want cigarettes what do you want?"

His father looked confused. "Huh? What the hell you talking about? What's at the store?"

"No, Dad. I'm asking you what you want from the store."

"Oh. Well, why didn't you say so? I'll take a candy bar. And none of that garbage with peanuts in it. The last time you got me one with peanuts in it, and they got in my teeth."

Dan squirmed in discomfort, because his father was breathing on him just inches from his face—the stench was overpowering. "Dad, I'm going to need some money."

His father dug into his pockets. "Oh sure, sure, money, everybody wants money." He pulled out a couple of crumpled twenty dollar bills and slapped them on the counter. Dan grabbed one of the bills and the garbage.

"OK, thanks. I'll be back."

"Wait, wait! Here, take this other one and get me some cigs will ya? Oh, and some beef jerky."

Dan smiled, took the twenty, and slipped out the door. He tossed the garbage in the dumpster and tucked the money in his pocket. He turned and spoke to his friend who wasn't there, "And that, my dear Mike, is how I always have money for those Toaster Tarts you're so fond of."

Dan broke out into a jog; it was a good mile and half to the hospital. He'd get the "groceries" on the way back. He was extremely worried that he couldn't reach anyone at the Deans. At this point he had no way of knowing the situation. The thoughts came in a rush, "What if Mr. Dean is dying? Or has brain damage? Maybe they're at his bedside? If that's the case, would they even want me there? If he's really dying, I want to tell him what he's meant to me. He should know that." The more he thought about it, the faster he ran.

Mike and Matt didn't know how good they had it, and he hoped it would stay that way. As the blocks slipped by he would take a quick look through the front window of the houses he passed. He could see people winding down their day, watching television, playing with their kids, reading the paper. It seemed so tranquil compared to the scene he had just left. He dreamed of one day having a house with large front windows where some snot-nosed kid like himself might go running by. But for now, the peace in Dan's life, his refuge of tranquility, was the Dean home, and Dan was feeling more than a little unsettled by the possibility that it could change.

Mr. Dean looked around his room. He was surprisingly awake. He knew he should be sleeping but just couldn't. Now that he was somewhat certain that he was going to live, the worry really started to set in. He had just gotten a great job, and now he knew there was no way they were going to retain him. They would need to fill the position soon. They couldn't wait for him to rehabilitate, let alone six weeks of bed rest. He lay in the hospital bed agonizing, not about his injuries, but how he was going to make the mortgage payment. Even if they were able to hold the ship above water for a couple of months, where was he going to get a job?

Chapter Twelve

Dark thoughts seeped in. "If I had gotten killed, my insurance would have set the family up for life. My wife wouldn't have to worry about money for the mortgage or how we were going to send the kids to college. Maybe I'll still croak, and it will work out."

He immediately chased away such thoughts. "What a sniveling little whiner you've become, Peter Dean. You just escaped the clutches of death, and you're complaining about a couple little problems. Buck up man. You'll solve the troubles as they reveal themselves. You're the luckiest man alive. You've got a great wife, two healthy, wonderful kids. It'll work out—As long as you're alive, you're still in the fight. Focus on solutions. Remember, 97% of our worries never come to pass."

He was glad that this moping and dwelling on the negative only occurred in his own head. Even though there wasn't anyone to witness it, he was still feeling embarrassed for his little pity party. He needed to go to sleep, or he needed a distraction. "Maybe I can convince the nurse to dial down the pain killers; if the pain occupies my time at least I'll be busy. Well… since I'm awake, I might as well start working on a battle plan. The boys could probably help me get out my resume to some other companies. This is going to be an all hands on deck endeavor."

Dan could see the hospital lights; he was just a couple of blocks away. When he was on the phone with the hospital, they said that the Intensive Care was closed for visits, but, to Dan that meant that the rest of the hospital still had visiting hours. If he could just get in, then he might be able to sneak onto Mr. Dean's floor and see what was going on. If nothing else, he could stop by the nurse's station and see if they had any information. He coasted into the hospital parking lot. Despite having run over a mile at a pretty good clip, he was feeling surprisingly OK. Apparently, practice had drubbed most of the toxins out of him. As he approached the large glass doors at the entrance of the hospital, he could see a receptionist and a security guard. "Gatekeepers! I'm going to need a different entrance."

He walked around the side of the hospital, trying every door. As he turned the corner he saw the signs for the Emergency Entrance. He thought that perhaps there might be enough chaos going on in the Emergency area that he could slip into another part of the hospital. He jogged up to the door and walked in. There were quite a few people in the waiting room, and the staff all seemed somewhat busy. Dan kept walking toward the bathroom and noticed double doors at the end of the hallway. He took a quick glance behind him. No one seemed to spot him and, without looking back again, he pushed open the doors into the main portion of the hospital. Fortunately, there was a hospital directory just a few feet inside the entryway.

"Cool. Now I just need to find a way up there." He walked past the cafeteria. There were only a couple of people cleaning up and the gift shop was closed. To his dismay, all hallways seemed to lead back to the front of the hospital where the receptionist and the security guard were camped out. "There's got to be another way up." He back tracked toward the cafeteria and down a hallway that he assumed led to the kitchen. "Well, it's worth a shot." As he approached the end of the hall, he spied his salvation, a stairwell heading up. He bounded up the steps to the third floor. He quietly and carefully opened the door to see what he was up against.

Apparently, Dan had stumbled into an area where dirty laundry and dishes were put until they were taken away to be cleaned. There didn't appear to be anyone around, so he stepped into the room. "OK, genius, you're on the third floor. Now what?" There was another set of double doors on the far side of the room. He stepped up to the window in the door to take a peek. "YIKES! I'm right behind the nurse's station." From where he was positioned

Chapter Twelve

he could see the door numbers on the first few rooms directly across the hallway. Mr. Dean's was the second room to the right of the nurse's encampment. Dan decided to sit tight and see if their rounds would take them away from the desk long enough for him to slip into Mr. Dean's room.

Dan observed them closely for several minutes; only two nurses appeared to be on duty. "Maybe I'd like to work in the medical field," he thought. "It would be cool to save people's lives." One of the nurses got up and left the station. Dan cracked the door open so that he could listen. Just then he caught a break; the phone rang and the other remaining nurse picked up. This was his opening. Staying low he quickly crab-walked out to the side of the nurse's desk. Dan took a quick peek to the right and could see the first nurse walking down the hall away from him. The nurse above him at the desk seemed to be tied up on the phone. He needed to wait until the nurse walking down the hall entered a room, and then he was home free. Just then, the ding of the elevator went off to his left—someone was getting off on this floor! If he stayed put he was dead duck. "Oops."

Staying low, Dan bolted for Mr. Dean's door; he hit the handle just as "whoever" was stepping off the elevator. He ducked inside and closed the door—it shut with more force than he would have liked. The nurse who was walking down the hall looked back, only to see another nurse walking from the elevator. Fortunately, the nurse coming off the elevator had been looking at the charts she was carrying. When she heard the door shut from Mr. Dean's room, she looked up to see the nurse walking down the hall. And the nurse on the phone looked up and assumed that the noise either came from the nurse down the hall or the nurse from the elevator. Dan couldn't have planned it better, if he tried. Dan waited a few seconds before looking in Mr. Dean's direction. When he did, he was shocked to see Mr. Dean looking right at him.

"What in the world is that boy up to?" Mr. Dean thought. Dan was out of breath, sweating and obviously hiding. Mr. Dean motioned for him to pull up a chair. He sat there looking at Dan, trying to imagine what kind of trouble would have him seeking refuge in a hospital room.

Dan scooted over a chair to the side of the bed and looked Mr. Dean over in the process. "Are you all right? I mean, are you going to live?"

Mr. Dean gave him a thumbs up.

"Whew, that's such a relief. I haven't heard anything since Officer Tuttle came and picked up Mike. I tried calling the house, but no one answered, and then I called here, and they said I couldn't get any information until tomorrow. But I wouldn't have been able to sleep, so I kind of snuck into the hospital and…"

Mr. Dean patted him on the shoulder as if to say, "It's all right. I understand."

Dan put his forehead down on the side of the bed, "I just wanted you to know how much you mean to me." Dan didn't want to choke up, but his voice betrayed him and broke with emotion.

Mr. Dean patted him on the head and, when Dan looked up, painfully nodded his head as if to say, "Me, too."

"How long do you need the tube down your throat?"

Mr. Dean shrugged and turned the palms of his hands up indicating, "I don't know."

"Have you seen Mike and Matt yet?"

Mr. Dean signaled a "thumbs down." It was difficult for Mr. Dean to make these movements because he was so sore, but it made him focus.

"Oh. OK, well, I won't tell them that I was here."

Mr. Dean pointed at the welt on Dan's right eye. Dan, in his haste, hadn't even noticed that the slug he received from his father had resulted in anything. "Oh, that. That's just from practice. As you can imagine, I didn't do very well."

Mr. Dean's smile was still partially visible beneath the medical tape. He knew that Dan was probably pretty sick at practice.

They went on "chatting" like this for several minutes, until Dan excused himself, so that Mr. Dean could sleep. Mr. Dean shook Dan's hand with both of his own hands and held onto his grip to let Dan know that he appreciated him coming by. Dan waved before exiting, and Mr. Dean did the same.

As the door closed, Mr. Dean thought about how touching it was for Dan to have gone to such lengths to come check on him. He cared for Dan and had high hopes for him, he knew the upcoming years were going to be a challenge to keep Dan on the right path. But, for the moment, he felt good that he was making a difference in Dan's life. Certainly, Dan's visit was a nice distraction. He had expended a lot of energy "talking" with Dan. Mr. Dean closed his eyes. "Maybe I can go to sleep after all."

Dan smiled at the nurses as the door closed behind him. "Have a good evening, Ladies." He walked to the elevators with a bounce in his step and smile on his face. "Mission accomplished."

CHAPTER 13

Matt and Mike were both anxious to see their dad. It had been decided the night before that they would stay home from school. As they tumbled downstairs, they could smell breakfast was already on the table. "Come on, Boys. I hope you're hungry." Entering the kitchen the kids were greeted with a feast the likes of which they had never seen.

"Wow, Mom! Look at all this stuff," Matt said.

Mike couldn't believe they were having blueberry pancakes AND French toast, bacon AND sausage, PLUS scrambled eggs, AND hash-browns with cheese. "Are there more people coming over?" he asked.

In addition to the main course, the table and counters were full with croissants, two kinds of muffins, fruit salad, yogurt, orange juice, AND grapefruit juice. Mrs. Dean turned from the sink and smiled at her children. "No. It's just us, but I thought with every-thing that happened yesterday, you guys deserved a treat. Besides, I was up early, and I can take some of the leftovers to your father—that hospital food is usually not that great."

Chapter Thirteen

"Your eyes are all red and puffy," Matt pointedly noted.

"Oh. That's probably just allergies."

Matt looked at Mike in a puzzled fashion. "But Mom, you don't have allergies."

Mrs. Dean put her hands on her hips. "Well, I'm allergic to your father being in the hospital. Now, eat up before everything gets cold."

Matt may have suspected, but Mike knew for certain—his mother had been up crying and probably started cooking because she couldn't sleep. He pulled out his chair and plopped down. He knew it was his job to stuff himself and be appreciative—a task both he and Matt were all too happy to complete.

Matt dug in with all the enthusiasm of a snow day. "Mom, can we watch a movie before we go to the hospital?"

"We'll see. It all depends on when your father is ready to see us."

Mr. Dean had slept soundly, but with the arrival of the morning came eye popping soreness. It was as if he had run a triathlon, lifted weights to complete exhaustion, and then played tackle football with guys that all weighed 350 pounds.

He flexed his hands and lifted his arms in an attempt to work out the discomfort by getting some blood moving. He repeated the process, lifting his arms higher each time, being careful not to displace the IV in his arm. As he lifted his arms above his head, the door opened and Dr. Roberts stepped in. "Well, what do we have here? Infirm aerobics?"

Mr. Dean sheepishly put his arms down.

"Oh, don't let me stop you, but I'm thinking we need to get you some deodorant, if you're going to continue working out like this. You might foul up the entire intensive care unit."

Mr. Dean appreciated the good natured "guy talk" ribbing; it made him feel that the worst was behind him.

"So how are you feeling today?" Mr. Dean gave the doctor a thumbs up. "I spoke with your wife yesterday—actually I spoke to you, too, but I don't think you remember. I'm Dr. Roberts. I did the surgery on your leg."

Mr. Dean nodded and stuck out his hand. Dr. Roberts chuckled and received a firm handshake from his patient, "Nice to meet you, too. From the nurse's comments you seem to be getting a good pulse in your leg which indicates that circulation is normal. Let me just look at a few things here."

Dr. Roberts checked the swelling and color in Mr. Dean's lower legs; he also tested for feeling and response on the leg that Mr. Dean broke. Everything looked normal for the first day after surgery. "OK. Looks good. As your wife may have explained, a couple of the concerns we have relate to clotting and infection. You had a compound break of your femur or thigh bone—and by compound, I mean that when you broke the largest bone in your body in half, it was sticking through your skin and created a fairly significant wound. We were able to put humpty dumpty back together again, and it should be fine. You also have a small break of your pelvis which will require bed rest to heal. Both of these injuries bleed quite a bit, so we had to put a few pints of blood in you. Of course, you also have some broken ribs and a collapsed lung, but, all in all, I'd say you're a very lucky guy."

Mr. Dean could tell that Dr. Roberts was wrapping up, so he pointed to the tube down his throat. "Ah, you'd like to get that out, huh?"

Chapter Thirteen

Mr. Dean nodded yes.

"OK. Let me take a listen." Dr. Roberts moved his stethoscope to different spots on Mr. Dean's chest. "Well, it sounds like progress. Let's get you a chest X-ray and, if that looks good, I'd say we could probably get that out for you early this afternoon, maybe just after lunch. Now, when they remove this, I want you to be thinking about a happy place and fight your gag reflex. We can't have you throwing up during the extraction; we need to avoid that potential setback. OK?"

Mr. Dean gave him the "OK" sign.

"All right, we're going to keep you in intensive care for today and possibly tomorrow, but after that we'll transfer you to a regular room." Mr. Dean nodded that he understood.

"Now you can get back to those aerobics."

Mr. Dean flashed a final "thumbs up" as Dr. Roberts was leaving and, in general, was encouraged with the evaluation. He was looking forward to getting the breathing tube out, so that he could talk to his kids. Now he just needed to get a note to the nurse so that she could tell his wife when to bring the kids in. He pressed the call button and then continued his "aerobics."

Mrs. Dean was busy putting away the food from the morning feast. She was freezing what she could and packing the refrigerator with the rest of the goodies. The boys were clearing the table and doing the dishes, when the phone call came in from the nurse. Matt was closest to the phone and picked up.

"Hello, Matthew's Pizza—we make it, you bake it."

For a moment, there was silence on the other end of the line.

114

NEARFALL:

"Umm, this is Memorial Hospital. Is this the Dean residence?"

Mrs. Dean looked at her son crossly, "Matthew!"

Matt spoke sweetly into the phone, "Yes, Ma'am, this is the Dean residence. Let me get my mother for you, Ma'am." Matt handed his mom the phone. "They'd like a deep dish pepperoni with extra cheese."

She gave him a stern look and pointed at the dishes. Mike had tried not to laugh, but couldn't help himself.

Mrs. Dean covered the phone. "Don't encourage him," but at the last moment she cracked, and a small smile betrayed her discipline.

Mike picked up on it immediately. "YOU smiled!"

Mrs. Dean waved him off, directing her attention to the phone. "This is Mrs. Dean." She listened as the nurse explained that her husband's breathing tube wouldn't come out until the early afternoon. "OK. Thank you. Yes, I understand. I was wondering; I'd like to cheer my husband up with a couple of his favorite treats. Would that be OK? Yes, it's food. OK, great. Thanks for the call. Bye."

Mike anxiously inquired, "Is everything all right with Dad?"

"Yes, everything is fine, but they are going to be doing some additional X-rays and other tests to make sure that his leg is in the right position. So, we're not going to be able to see him until this afternoon."

"Aww, man. What are we going to do until then?" Matt lamented.

Mrs. Dean thought for a moment before responding, "Well, since

115

Chapter Thirteen

I have at my disposal a couple of strapping young men, you two can help me get the house ready for when Dad comes home."

Mike surveyed the house. "What do you mean? The house is spotless."

Mrs. Dean continued, "Oh, I know. I did most of the cleaning this morning. Right now I need your strong backs." Matt and Mike looked at each other and shrugged, then looked back at their mother for further explanation. "Your father is not going to be able to climb stairs for several weeks, so I need you to help me move our bedroom downstairs."

Matt immediately complained, "I thought we were going to watch a movie?"

His mother countered, "I said 'maybe.' Besides it's such a beautiful day. You boys should go outside and play basketball or something."

Matt immediately took off for the back door. Mrs. Dean qualified her remarks. "AFTER you help me."

Matt took his hand off the doorknob. "I was that close to freedom." He looked back at his mother. "You know, Mom, my back isn't that strong. I'm little and feeble. But Mike, he's your guy. I mean he's a wrestler, he lifts weights; he'd probably do it just for a workout. I could maybe go sweep out the garage or something. Besides, I think in school they said I shouldn't lift anything heavy until I was much older."

Mike stood with his hands on his hips, just waiting to voice a rebuttal, on the off chance his mother was swayed by his brother's nonsense. Mrs. Dean smiled at Matt. "That's a great idea; you can sweep the garage—after you help your brother and me." She continued with a mocking tone, "Personally, I think any boy that gets into a fight with a big kid a year older than him and handles himself SO bravely can probably handle himself moving a few items."

Matt didn't miss a beat. "Well, that's another thing; I'm still recovering from my injuries. I probably shouldn't strain myself."

Mrs. Dean stopped smiling. "Matthew Dean, you've already negotiated yourself into sweeping the garage; would you like to clean the car too?"

Matt's gusto promptly evaporated. "No, Ma'am."

Kimberly was working her way through the lunch line when she felt a hand on her shoulder; she turned to look over her shoulder—it was TJ.

"Looks like I'm free for lunch today, so I'm glad you'll be joining me."

Kimberly scoffed and shrugged his hand off her shoulder. "In your dreams."

TJ looked at her menacingly, "You don't really think I'm going to let anyone be with you…you're mine. It's just a matter of time."

"My goodness, you're so clever. That almost rhymed."

Kimberly picked up her lunch, leaving TJ surrounded by tittering classmates. Despite appearing to be in complete control as she put TJ in his place, Kimberly walked to her table worried. "Why can't this guy take a hint?"

Mr. Dean was so relieved to have the breathing tube out that he felt he might burst if he didn't talk to somebody. The process of having the tube removed was no picnic and not one that Mr. Dean would recommend. However, now that it was out, he couldn't believe how much he missed being able to speak.

He hummed a few bars of some favorite songs. He couldn't carry much of tune, but he tried out his vocals on some old Elvis songs. He decided to go back to humming, after a stabbing pain reminded him that he still had broken ribs. His early morning "total body" soreness had diminished, but he was feeling uncomfortable from not being able to shift to his side or move around much. His broken leg was aching, but that was to be expected. After hearing Dr. Roberts's description he was actually surprised that it didn't hurt more. He decided to try whistling, just as the nurse was walking into his room.

"Ah, sorry. I apparently have become enamored with my rediscovered vocal ability."

"Yes, I know. The other nurses and I really enjoyed your rendition of Blue Suede Shoes. We're all pitching in for lessons."

Mr. Dean was a little embarrassed. "Sorry. I didn't realize I was that loud."

The nurse smiled, "Oh, you weren't loud, but, in your enthusiasm, you apparently hit your call button. We didn't have the heart to interrupt you."

Mr. Dean was mortified, but his nurse let him off the hook. "Don't feel bad. You lightened up an otherwise slow day."

Mr. Dean recovered his stride. "Well, I thought a free concert might earn me a hospital discount."

NEARFALL:

The nurse was checking his vital signs, but, despite being distracted, had a sharp wit and seemed to enjoy the banter. "Well, you should apply for that. If nothing else, they could give you a royalty on all the business you're driving to the ear doctors and mental health practitioners."

Mr. Dean laughed out loud, but that was cut abruptly short by sharp pain.

"OK, Mr. Dean, you need to take it easy. I'm not sure if you're aware, but you were in a nasty car accident."

Before Mr. Dean could respond, the door opened and Matt burst into the room. "Dad!" Mr. Dean held up his hand. "Whoa, Partner! Slow down."

Matt broke stride. "Don't worry, Dad. I wasn't going to jump on you."

"Well, it's not that I don't want you to. It's just that I'm little under the weather right now. Come here, and let me take a look at you."

Matt walked over to the edge of the bed, and his Dad put his arm around him. "You know, if your face wasn't so bruised, you'd be a pretty good-looking kid."

Matt's bruising had started to turn a sickening yellow mixed in with various shades of purple. "Well, you shouldn't beat me."

Mr. Dean looked at the nurse. "He's kidding." The nurse walked to the door. "It's hard to imagine where he got his sarcasm from. Your vitals are good. Just check off what you'd like to eat this evening on the menu, and I'll be back to pick it up in a few minutes."

"OK. Will do. Thank you."

Chapter Thirteen

Mr. Dean turned his attention back to Matthew. "You're a witty guy, but you need to be careful with some of your jokes. This is a hospital, and they get kids in here that have been hurt by their parents, so you need to be a little sensitive to that—got me?"

"Yeah, I understand, but it was a little funny wasn't it?"

Mr. Dean chuckled, "Yeah, it was moderately amusing. Where's your mom and Mike?"

Matt was looking over the monitors attached to his father, "Mom had to stop at the desk, and Mike went to the gift shop to get a card."

Mrs. Dean opened the door. "There's my beautiful wife," Mr. Dean said with zeal, "What's with all the packages?"

Mrs. Dean emptied her arms onto a chair, "Well, I couldn't sleep and I kind of went nuts cooking. I brought some of it with me, in case you got hungry."

"That's just some of it?" Mr. Dean responded.

"Yeah, like I said, I went a little overboard."

"Well, stop fussing with that, and come over here so I can give my wife a kiss."

Mrs. Dean walked over and gave Mr. Dean a lingering kiss. Mr. Dean held her hand, "I'm really glad I'm still able to do that."

Matt rolled his eyes. "You guys are getting too mushy already."

"Oh, hush," Mrs. Dean directed, "and go see if your brother is in the hallway."

NEARFALL:

Matt stuck his head out the door. Mike was just coming off the elevator. Matt motioned for him, and Mike waved back. "He's coming off the elevator now," Matt said as he ducked back into the room. "So, how long do you have to stay in here, Dad?"

"The doctor said I'll need to be in this room for a day or two more, but I'm not sure how long I'll be in the hospital."

Mike walked into the room with his card in his hand. "Hey, Dad, how are you feeling?"

"I'm all right, Michael. How are you doing?" Mike thought it was a silly question, considering the circumstances.

"Me? I'm all right; I'm not the one that was in a car accident."

Matt chimed in, "Yeah, Dad, we saw your car. It was burnt and all smashed."

Mr. Dean looked up at his wife. "Burned?"

"Yeah, the kids thought you would be burned, because they saw your car on the news when they pulled it from the bottom of the hill."

 Mr. Dean thought for moment. "Well, I remember smelling gas, but I'm pretty sure that the car wasn't burning when I was pulled out."

Mike handed his Dad the card he purchased. "This is for you."

"Hey thanks, Buddy. Should I open it now, or would you rather I open it later?"

"Later would be better," Michael said, sounding relieved.

"OK. Well, I'll just put that over here then." Mr. Dean set the card on the table next to the bed.

Chapter Thirteen

Matt was looking at the machine bubbling next to the bed with a tube leading up to his dad's chest. "What's this thing for?"

"Well, when I had the accident all the air was pushed out of this lung, so they're slowly pumping it back up, so I can breathe normally," Mr. Dean explained.

"Can you feel it?" Mike asked.

"Yeah, Dad, what does it feel like?" Matt added.

"I don't really feel anything; it just hurts a little bit when I move," Mr. Dean replied.

"We were worried about you Dad." Mike looked away from his father as he made the statement, as if afraid to admit that he was scared.

"Yeah, I'm sorry about that guys. I certainly didn't mean to worry you. I just didn't see that deer until the last instant, and I swerved to miss it."

"Oh, so that's what happened?" Mrs. Dean asked. "I had asked the police officer, but he didn't know. They thought you might have fallen asleep or swerved to miss oncoming traffic."

"No, it was big buck. I swerved, and I just got too far over on the shoulder."

"You should have hit it," Matt offered. "We could have had venison steak for a month."

"Well, Matthew, in retrospect, you're probably right."

Mr. Dean looked at his wife. "Why did you need to stop at the desk?"

Mrs. Dean rolled her eyes. "Oh just some insurance stuff." Mr.

NEARFALL:

Dean tensed his jaw and gave his wife a knowing look. He knew she was stressed about what this was going to do to their financial situation.

"We can talk about that later. I've been thinking about a plan." Mrs. Dean squeezed her husband's hand. "Don't you worry about it. You just focus on getting better. The most important thing is that we still have our family all together—we'll deal with the rest of it later." Mr. Dean was thankful for his wife's support, but he hated worrying her.

His anxiety was interrupted by a knock at the door. The nurse poked her head in. "Is it all right if I come in for a second?"

Mrs. Dean stepped away from the bed. "Yes, of course. We'll get out of your way."

The nurse responded, "Oh, that's OK. I've already checked him. I just wanted to let you know that there is a gentleman here to see you. Normally, we have strict rules about visitation on this floor, but the hospital administrator thought it would be OK. Your wife will need to go back down to admitting after and sign some forms."

Mr. Dean looked at his wife; she shrugged as if to say, "I have absolutely no idea." Mr. Dean looked back at the nurse. "Well, send this mystery man in."

The nurse went back out into the hallway, and in stepped Jack Ross, the guy that had hired Mr. Dean. The boys and Mrs. Dean were utterly confused, and Mr. Dean was stunned for a moment. "Uh, Honey, this is Jack Ross. He's the gentleman that was kind enough to offer me a job. Jack, this is my wife, Diane, and my kids, Michael and Matthew."

Jack shook Mrs. Dean's hand and said hello to the boys. "Peter, I must say, you were looking a little better when I saw you last."

Chapter Thirteen

Mr. Dean played the comment off, "Well, I just wasn't feeling challenged in my life, so..."

Mr. Ross continued, "That's what we were supposed to take care of for you. You didn't have to go and get all noble and try to add on some extra burdens—which brings me to my point. I'd like to correct what you stated just a moment ago. You said that I offered you a job, but it is my recollection that you accepted that job and filled out the paperwork that proves it. That being said, as an employee of our humble little company, you're on the same insurance plan as the rest of us. I took the liberty of having Cheryl in Human Resources call the hospital and take care of everything. However, I think your wife will need to sign a couple of forms for the hospital."

Mrs. Dean squeezed her husband's hand. She was trying not to be emotional, especially in front of the kids, but it was such a huge relief she couldn't keep her eyes from welling up. Mr. Ross added, "Of course we know you're going to be laid up for little while. I could only get you three-fourths pay until you return to work full time. We'd like to get you set up on a speaker phone so you can be in on all the meetings, and, naturally we're going to bury you in study materials. So, once you get settled in at home, we'll get you started, if that sounds OK to you?"

Mr. Dean was bowled over. "Yes, of course. That'll be great. I'll do everything I can to get up to speed."

Jack glanced at his watch. "All righty, then. That settles that. You just get busy healing. I don't want to take any more of your time, and I'm here on a short leash from the hospital. I just wanted to come by and let you know that we don't accept this accident as means for you to wiggle out of that contract you signed. Mrs. Dean, it was nice to have met you. Boys, take it easy on your dad. It'll be a little while before he can get after you."

NEARFALL:

Mrs. Dean wiped away her tears. "Thank you, Mr. Ross. I like your company already."

"Well it's OUR company now, Ma'am, and we're very pleased to have your husband working with us."

Mr. Dean shook hands with Mr. Ross. "Thanks, Jack. I won't let you down."

"I know you won't Peter." Mr. Ross gave everyone a wave good-bye and slipped out the door.

Mrs. Dean smiled at her husband and looked at her watch. "Well, I'd better get down there and see what forms they need me to sign before they go home for the day."

Mr. Dean returned her smile. "Yes, you'd better."

She gave her husband a kiss. "You must have given one heck of interview."

"Hey, what I can tell you? I'm really good one-on-one."

Mrs. Dean walked to the door. "OK, Guys, stay here with your father, I'll be right back."

Matt, lobbed a request, "Can I have root beer?"
"I'll see what I can do." Mrs. Dean answered. "Michael do you want anything?"
"I'll have a root beer, too, if they have it." Mike responded.

Mrs. Dean left the room and Mr. Dean fell back into his pillow with one thought, "97% of our fears never happen."

CHAPTER 14

Mike was at his locker grabbing his books for homeroom, when Dan spied him. Dan was still on the other end of the hallway and picked up the pace so that he could chat with Mike before the bell. Mike closed his locker and started to turn down the hall toward class. "Hey, Mike, wait up."

Mike turned to see Dan loping down the corridor. They had a special handshake they did when they greeted one another.

"Hey, my brother from a different mother, how's your dad doing?"

"He's going to be OK. He's got a broken leg and some broken ribs, but the doctors say he should be fine."

Dan looked relieved. "So can he talk?"

Mike looked at Dan like he'd just taken a stupid pill. "What does a broken leg have to do with him talking? Yes, he can talk—of course he can talk. Why would you think he wouldn't be able to talk?"

NEARFALL:

Dan tried to recover. He had told Mr. Dean that he wouldn't tell Mike that he had been up to the hospital. "I don't know, you see on television when people get in bad wrecks, they sometimes can't talk for a while, I didn't know if he had been hit in the head or whatever."

Mike seemed to be satisfied with the answer. "No, he's fine, just a few broken bones."

Dan exhaled loudly, "That's a load off my mind. I've been worried sick. I tried calling you a few times, but I couldn't reach anyone. You guys need to get an answering machine."

They turned into their homeroom, and Mike laughed, "You say that like you're basking in the glow of an answering machine yourself. You still have a black rotary dial phone from the Stone Age."

Dan easily redirected the jab, "Hey, I don't need an answering machine. NOBODY calls ME."

Mike felt badly as he took his seat behind Dan. "Hey, I'm sorry about that. I didn't call last night because we stayed up at the hospital until they kicked us out, and the night before we went out to eat with my grandparents. You know my grandpa. He can tell stories until the crack of dawn, so I didn't get home until really late. I figured your dad was in his room by then."

Dan debated whether he should take a couple more shots at making his buddy feel guilty, but the bell rang. "Hey, don't worry about it, Bud. I'm just glad your dad is going to be OK."

Matt returned to school feeling pretty good about the world. The thing with his dad was a big scare, and he was very thankful that everything worked out. It certainly helped put things in perspective. His problem with TJ seemed rather minor in the grand scheme of things. Matt took a measure of comfort knowing that Mr. Merrill was now on the case. He resolved not to worry about it anymore and just let it go.

As Matt entered his classroom it was apparent that someone had called the school and let them know that his father was OK. He had just walked through the door when Mrs. Wilson approached him and told him how glad she was to hear that his dad would make a complete recovery.

Matt spent most of the morning sharing the story of the accident with his classmates. "Sorry to hear about your dad," notes would be slipped to him; he'd scribble a few lines and a quick thank you before sending the note back through the ranks. However, it wasn't until just prior to lunch that he received the note he had been hoping for. He opened Kimberly's note and felt his pulse quicken. "I've been worried about you. Will you sit with me at lunch?" Matt looked over at Kimberly. She had been watching him read her message. He nodded "yes," and they both smiled with anticipation.

Jerry Rusk just couldn't shake the idea of knowing what became of Mr. Dean. After he had been interviewed by the state patrol, he didn't have time to visit the hospital. He still had a job to do and needed to deliver his cargo to California. After a day on the road, he decided not to follow up. He didn't want to get emotionally involved. "If the guy didn't make it, I'd rather not know." It was better to just imagine that Mr. Dean survived and would lead a productive life. But now, as his truck was being unloaded and the prospect of heading back to Iowa was upon him, he had a change of heart. He had tried for the better part of three days to put the scene out of his mind, but it kept creeping back in. He realized that to have some finality, he needed to know the result—good or bad. Now that he had made up his mind, he was anxious to get back on the road. The sooner he could get back to Iowa, the sooner he could put this whole thing behind him. At least that was the hope.

Mike was nearly late to Mr. Rhenkin's class. It was always a challenge, because he had to go from the gym which was located on the far end of the building to the second floor on the opposite end of the school. It would be manageable, but his gym teacher was a stickler for making sure everyone showered. Mike had protested this formal procedure, but it was awkward to be very forceful in his dissent—his gym teacher was his wrestling coach. When he lodged his complaint, Coach McCreary simply stated that for some of the kids, it would be the only shower they took that day. Despite the inconvenience, he expected Mike to deal with it. This often meant that Mike would run from gym to Mr. Rhenkin's class arriving in a pool of sweat—undoing what his shower was to have solved.

However, today's gym class was dance, and they weren't required to shower. Mike was simply dreading having to see Billy. He shuddered at what his list of possible demands might be. As Michael entered class, Dan paused his full court press of Vanessa long enough to give Mike a "what's up" head-bob. Mike was glad that Dan seemed to have distanced himself from the other girls that he had gotten drunk with.

Vanessa was hot, but she had a good head on her shoulders. It was better to have Dan putting his efforts in her direction. Mike took his seat as Mr. Rhenkin began to take roll. Billy reached back and tossed a note on Mike's desk. Mike looked at it with dismay. He slowly unfolded it and read the contents. "Meet me at Pattison Park after your wrestling practice." Billy looked over his shoulder, and Mike nodded an acknowledgement.

Pattison Park was on his way home and right near his brother's grade school. Mike put the note in his pocket. "Great—something to look forward to."

Chapter Fourteen

Matt had recounted the story of the accident to Kimberly in great detail as they ate lunch together. She had wanted him to sit next to her, and he did as she requested, but he felt uneasy. He definitely liked being close to her, but it was difficult to talk to her. He had to turn sideways to see her face, and gauge her reaction to what he was saying. Plus, he had so many other things going on in his head—his mother's voice mostly. "Sit up straight. Don't chew with your mouth open. Don't talk with food in your mouth. Keep your elbows off the table." These things that previously had held little importance in Matt's life now had great implication—he was trying to impress a girl. All the social graces plus trying to be entertaining was a lot of pressure.

Matt suddenly got the feeling that someone was looking at him. He scanned the lunch room, but didn't see anyone glancing his way. Matt turned to look behind him, but Kimberly reached out and touched his arm. "Don't give him the satisfaction." At once Matt realized why Kimberly positioned their "date" as she had. She knew that TJ would be skulking behind them. Matt was impressed with her preparation, and he gave her a smile. "You're really something Kimberly Johnson." Kimberly batted her eyes before responding, "I'm glad you think so, Matthew Dean."

Dan waited for Mike in the hallway as Mr. Rhenkin's class let out. They walked a few paces to make sure they were out of earshot of anyone.

"So what was on Pudgeball's list of punishments? Will you be wearing a French maid's outfit? Or can he be bought off with a toga and quart of olive oil?"

Mike rolled his eyes. "Ha, ha, ha. No, he just said to meet him at Pattison Park after practice."

Dan was unrelenting. "Well, maybe he'll be bringing the togas."

Mike chuckled, "Would you shut up? I'm sure he just wants me to join the chess club or play dungeons and dragons with him. He's not that bad. He's just a lonely kid, but I'm glad to know my pain is bringing you such amusement."

Dan changed tack, "You're right, Mike, I'm sorry. Do you want me to go with you—for back-up?"

Mike looked at Dan disbelievingly. "No, I'll be fine."

Dan just couldn't leave it alone. "All right, Man, I'm off to gym, but when Billy's slowly skinning your hide for a new lamp shade collection, just remember, I offered to go with you."

Mike laughed. "You're a dork."

Matt met Kimberly after school. They had decided at lunch that Matt would walk Kimberly part of the way home. Kim was talking to a couple of her friends as Matt approached. He still couldn't get over how pretty and sweet she was. He also didn't know how to define this budding romance. His parents certainly would not condone actual dating—nor could he really call her his girlfriend. Matt dismissed the thoughts, "Hey I'm walking her home. I'm not marrying her…at least not yet."

Kimberly's friends scattered as Matt announced his arrival, "Hi, Kimberly." She waved to her friends and handed Matt her books. Matt hadn't realized that was part of the bargain. He had his own heavy book bag to carry, but he dutifully tucked her books under his arm.

As they strolled down the block, Kimberly told him about her trip to the Wisconsin Dells and all the amazing water slides she had gone on. "We're going there next summer. Maybe your parents will let you come with me?"

Chapter Fourteen

Matt had no idea how his parents would respond to such a proposal. "Yeah, that sounds like a lot of fun. They might let me go. I could ask them when we get closer to summer."

They walked in silence for a while, and Matt was scrambling to come up with conversation. Before he could settle on a topic, Kimberly reached out and grabbed his hand. Matt immediately got butterflies. "Holy mackerel, I'm holding hands with Kimberly Johnson! A week ago she wouldn't give me the time of day."

Kimberly asked, "What do you want to be when you grow up?"

Matt hadn't thought about the question for a long time. "I think I'd like to be a cop, a detective probably. How about you?"

Kimberly laid out a detailed dissertation on the pros and cons of her two choices: either a doctor or a singer. Matt jumped in when she finally came up for a breath, "Well, you seem to have given it a lot of thought. I'm sure you'll be great at either one."

They were approaching the alley where they needed to part ways. Kim asked one final question, "Have you ever kissed a girl, Matthew?"

Matt was floored by the question but tried to play it off. "Yeah, I've kissed a girl before." Kimberly looked disappointed until Matt added, "…my mom, my grandma, my aunt."

Kimberly smiled, put her hands on either side of his face, and kissed him. At first, Matt was so shocked he didn't close his eyes, but as the kiss hung on to the passing seconds, he closed his eyes. Kimberly pulled her head back slowly and opened her eyes. Matt was still pursing his lips and had his eyes closed. "You can open your eyes now." Matt smiled from ear to ear and opened one eye, then the other. "You're silly. Don't look at me with that big grin like the cat that ate the canary." She took her books out his hand, "I'll see you tomorrow Matthew Dean."

Matt just stood there smiling; finally he spoke, "Goodbye, Miss Johnson."

Matt turned down the alley as Kimberly headed up the block. His legs were unsteady, and his heart was racing. "Wow! Now, that's a nice end to a school day!" He was giddy; he had certainly never felt anything like this before. As the alley spilled back out to the pavement of another street, Matt took a left and headed for home. Just as a reflex he glanced both directions for traffic.

There weren't any cars, but roughly two blocks away he could see TJ and his cronies on bikes pedaling fast in Matt's direction. "Yikes!" Matt hit the gas, and ran as fast as his legs would carry him. He had a block to go to make it home. As he sprinted, he tried to make the calculation in his head about whether two blocks on a bike equaled one block running flat out. Matt was chugging for all he was worth, but his book bag was slowing him down. As he whizzed by his neighbors fenced yard, he tossed it over the cedar points at the top of the fence.

He could hear TJ gaining. "You're dead meat, Worm!" Matt turned the corner into his front yard. Bike tires screeched across the pavement as the brakes were applied. Matt leapt the front steps, opened the front door, and slammed it behind him. He got the deadbolt turned just as TJ reached the steps. "Come on out here, you little maggot!" Matt stuck his tongue out, made a "beep, beep" sound like the road runner, and walked into the house.

His mom was in the kitchen. "Matthew, how many times have I told you not to slam the front door when you come in? Goodness, you shook the entire house."

Chapter Fourteen

"Sorry, Mom." Matt plodded upstairs. "Looks like I'm going to need those wrestling lessons after all."

Mike met Billy as instructed after practice. Mike took a look around the park. It was nearly dark, and they were alone. "OK, Billy, so you've got me here. What's up?" Mike had no idea what to expect, especially with Dan's active imagination planting all manner of nonsense in Mike's head.

"I'm sorry to hear about your dad. Is he going to be OK?"

Mike was surprised by Billy's empathy. "Yeah, he's going to be fine, but thanks for asking."

"I'm glad to hear that. My dad died when I was in grade school, so I know how scary it can be to see your dad in the hospital."

Mike hadn't known that Billy's father had died. In an instant he was much more sympathetic to Billy's dorkiness. Billy stepped toward him. "So anyhow, here's the deal. I'm tired of people mocking me and ridiculing me. You're going to make them stop."

Mike raised his eyebrows in curiosity. "How am I going to do that exactly?" Billy was pacing, which was making Mike restless. "Billy, before you answer, can you just stand there and talk to me? I feel like I'm watching tennis match—back and forth, back and forth."

Billy stopped and looked directly at Mike. "I want you to hang out with me. I want you to have lunch at my table. I want you to acknowledge me in the hallway the same way you acknowledge other friends. I want you to defend me when people tease me, and I want you to talk me up around other cool people that you know. In short, I want to fit in. I'm not looking to date the hottest girl in school or be the most popular guy. I'm shooting for acceptance. And you're my ticket."

NEARFALL:

Mike looked at Billy. "So basically you're asking me to be your friend?"

"Well, yes, sort of, in all outward appearances—yes, that's exactly what I want people to think."

Mike paused to gather his thoughts. "Well, I don't know Billy—I'm not as cool as you think I am. Let's say, for the sake of argument, that I'm at least marginally cool and you're, well, you. I'd say there's a good chance that our hanging out together will just average to two dorky guys, both of whom will be uncool."

Billy smirked, "That's a chance I'm willing to take, or, of course I can just ask Mr. Rhenkin to do a side by side of our tests, along with my accusation of you cheating."

Mike knew that could get him kicked off the wrestling team, and unfortunately Billy knew it too. "I could just deny it."

Billy nodded in agreement, "That's true, but is that really a chance you want to take? I can be fairly convincing." Billy was resolute in tone and demeanor.

Mike had already been pondering coming clean and taking the punishment even without the looming threat of Billy ratting him out, so the threat didn't carry quite as much weight as Billy hoped it would. However, the proposition that Billy had put in front of him seemed intriguing. "All right, Billy, if I agree to this little plot, what are you willing to do?"

Billy looked at him puzzled. "Me? What am I willing to do?"

Mike was finding his groove. "Look, Billy, if I'm going to help you, you need to be willing to do what I say."

Chapter Fourteen

Billy hadn't considered the possibility that he might need to make some changes. He figured just being seen with Mike and his friends would be enough—cool by association. "What would I have to do?"

Mike certainly didn't consider himself a makeover consultant, but with Billy there were some easy fixes. "Who cuts your hair?"

Billy hesitated, "I do."

Mike looked at him dumbfounded. "Why?"

"Because when I was four, the barber got distracted and cut a chunk out of my ear, it bled all over the place. So I sort of have a phobia."

Mike tried to be understanding. "OK, well, let's change the scenario. Instead of a barbershop and some old codger cutting your hair, we'll take you to a salon and set you up with a very attentive FEMALE stylist."

Billy smiled at the thought of a young woman cutting his hair; being 13 he immediately imagined she was a supermodel with a pair of scissors. It sounded fine right up to the scissors part. "I don't know if that would work," Billy answered.

Mike continued to paint the picture. "I'm telling you, it's great. All of sudden you're being attended to like royalty. Her hands guide your head back over the sink. The warm water has never felt so good. She tenderly washes your hair and gently massages your scalp before she even cuts a single hair. You're going to love it."

Mike, of course, got his hair cut at a barbershop with his dad. He had gone to a salon once, before school pictures, and the woman that did the chopping was old enough to be his grandmother. Mike didn't see the harm playing into Billy's imagination if it helped him leave behind his fear…and his bowl cut.

Billy agreed to the salon trip. "What else?"

Mike looked Billy over. "Can you wear contacts?"

Billy shook his head no. "I have an astigmatism."

Mike was undeterred. "OK, we'll need to get a different style frame and do something about your wardrobe."

Billy protested, "My family doesn't have a lot of money. My mom is the only one that has a job. Besides, you can't make me into one of your jock friends."

Mike shifted gears. "Billy, I'm not talking about a lot of money. It doesn't take an expensive wardrobe. Look at my buddy, Dan. He's has four T-shirts, a couple pair of jeans, and the chicks dig him."

Billy scoffed, "Yeah, but that's because he was born a muscle-bound moron. He could wear rags, and they'd love him."

Mike was irritated by this appraisal. "Well, you've got Dan all wrong. First of all, Dan wasn't born with big muscles. He was skinny kid that started lifting weights, because he was tired of getting beat up by his dad."

Billy shifted uneasily on his feet; he had never considered the possibility that having a bad father could be worse than not having a father at all. "I'm sorry. I didn't know."

Mike softened his tone. "You don't like it when people prejudge you, be careful not to do the same." Billy nodded in agreement.

137

Chapter Fourteen

Mike had a flash of insight. "You know Billy, talking about Dan has given me a great idea. I can solve all your problems in one fell swoop."

Billy was curious. "OK, I'll bite. What is this magic bullet solution?"

Mike jumped up on first couple steps of the nearby slide. "You ready? Join the wrestling team!"

Billy's face dropped. "Is this a joke to you?"

"No, I'm serious, Billy; this accomplishes everything you're hoping for. Wrestlers stick together. There's sort of a brotherhood. Maybe because it's so hard, I don't know, but its there."

Billy wasn't buying it. "Look, that's fine for you and Dan, but I'm not an athlete, I'm the kid that always got picked last on the playground. I'm not a jock."

Mike responded enthusiastically, "You see, that's the beauty of it. You don't have to be jock. Wrestling is more than just pure athletic ability. It's about technique and strategy. You play chess, don't you?" Billy nodded, and Mike continued, "Wrestling is human chess. Imagine Billy, instead of talking about Greek gods wrestling, you'll be learning the modern day version of what it's like to be a gladiator."

Billy interrupted, "Well, gladiators were Romans, not Greeks."

Mike brushed it off, "OK then, a modern day warrior. You'll learn the techniques that date back to the original Olympians."

Billy was warming up to the idea. "It doesn't change the fact that I'd be looked at like a dweeb."

NEARFALL:

Mike was trying to handle Billy's objections. "Hey, I'm not telling you won't take some lumps at first. There will be guys on the team that'll give you a hard time for being there, but what do you care?"

Billy shrugged. "I don't see how that improves things."

"You're missing the point Billy. If you can prove that you can withstand wrestling practice day after day, you'll have the respect you're looking for. "Cool" on the wrestling team is all based on merit. We've got rich kids, poor kids, cool kids, nerd kids, but we're all wrestlers. In the wrestling room no one cares what car your parents drive, what clothes you wear, or if the student body at large thinks you're cool. Look at Dan, his dad is an alcoholic, and they live in a run-down trailer park, but on that team Dan is respected, because he outworks everyone. He finishes practice and runs home. He lifts weights every night. He's the best, and that carries over to the rest of the school, because everyone knows not to mess with wrestlers."

Billy was starting to buy in. "What if I'm always horrible?"

Mike quickly answered, "It won't matter that you weren't a born jock. Wrestling gives you the tools to overcome your limitations. It might take you longer than other guys, but if you practice, you'll continue to improve. You didn't just sit down at a chess board for the first time and expect to be good, did you? I'm telling you, Billy, all you need to do is survive practice, and you'll have forty guys that will go to bat for you. It's everything that you said you wanted, and the best part is that you'll have earned it."

Billy sat down on the merry-go-round and looked at Mike. "You should go into sales."

CHAPTER 15

The reddish brown sandstone edifice of their school was not nearly as difficult to wear down as getting Dan to come sit with Billy at lunch. Dan, it seemed, was having a harder time buying into Mike's "project" than Billy was. Although Billy hadn't participated in a practice yet, he did get his physical and convince his mother to sign the release form. From Billy's description of his protective mother, it took a sales pitch equal to Mike's own. "Not bad for a two day commitment," Mike thought. In the meantime, Mike brought his coach on board with the Billy venture and worked out permission to have Matt watch practice. Matt was too young to participate with the team, but Coach McCreary would allow Mike to work with Matt for 15 minutes after practice. Mike had been sitting with Billy at lunch for two days in a row, and Billy was enjoying having someone to talk to. Usually Billy sat by himself.

As Mike and Dan headed for the lunch room, Mike continued to grind on Dan. "What are you too good to sit with another human being? You can't sit with me, because you're scared Billy might bring your status down? Is your ego really that fragile? Oh my, the great Dan Morgan can only be seen with the cool people that smoke blunt."

Dan put an elbow in Mike's side. "Hey, back off me." Mike could see Dan was getting mad, but pleading hadn't worked; now Mike was resorting to shame. Dan stopped in the hallway and pointed a finger at Mike. "Be careful how far you push this."

Mike felt his own jolt of anger. "Are you threatening me? Because if you are, you know where to find me." Mike knew Dan could turn him inside out, but he wasn't going to let his friend back him down.

Dan sized Mike up and caved first. He knew that he could beat Mike to a pulp, but he loved Mike's resolve. Dan smiled, "Ah man, shut-up. OK, let's go sit with the four-eyed powder puff."

Mike breathed a sigh of relief. "Whew, for a second there I thought you were going to guns on me."

Dan looked at Mike as they picked up their trays. "I'm doing this under protest and on one condition: I'm telling this kid exactly what I think of him and exactly what to expect when he gets to practice. I know you've been glossing over how difficult this is going to be for our young butterball. In fact, I'll bet you two boxes of Toaster Tarts he doesn't make it through three practices before he quits."

Mike agreed to the terms. "I'll take that bet."

Billy was already sitting at the table as Mike and Dan worked their way through the lunch line. Billy had found a book in the library on basic wrestling moves. He was shocked to see how many moves there were. The book was nearly two inches thick— and this was just supposed to be the basics. "I can see why Mike was drawing the comparison to chess."

Chapter Fifteen

Mike and Dan made their way to the table. Mike knew that his sitting with Billy caused a little ripple, but Dan sitting with Billy was going to be a major wave in the rumor mill. Billy took a sip of his coke as Mike and Dan sat down. Mike sat next to Billy and Dan directly across from him. Billy was more than a little shocked.

Mike handled the introductions. "I know you guys know each other, but I don't know that you've ever been formally introduced, Billy Johnson, this is Dan Morgan." Dan stuck out his hand and Billy shook it like a limp noodle.

"OK Johnson, I hear you're coming out for the wrestling team, is that correct?"

Billy looked at Mike and then back at Dan. "Yes, today is my first day of practice."

Dan looked Billy in the eyes. "Look, I'm telling you this for your own good. You're the softest kid I've ever seen in my life. I've seen room temperature sticks of butter with more muscle tone than you. You need to prepare yourself for unimaginable pain. You are going to get pounded on. I'm not trying to be mean or to scare you, I'm just attempting to get your mind ready. I've been wrestling for several years, but each year I am so sore after the first few days of practice I can hardly get out of bed in the morning. You need to gear up for that."

Billy looked like he might quit right there at the lunch table. "So you're saying it's not like chess?"

Dan looked at Mike. "Is that what you've been telling him? Yeah, it's like chess, except the bishop and the knight get to checkmate by turning you into a pretzel."

Billy was surprised that Dan knew the names of chess pieces.

NEARFALL:

"Maybe he's not as dumb as I thought?" He decided to risk the ultimate question, "Are you saying it's a mistake for me to go out for this team?"

Dan looked at Mike and then back at Billy. "No, I'm saying this is going to be more difficult than you can even imagine right now. You need to understand that every day you're going to want to quit, and every single day you need to talk yourself into staying.

Billy looked confused. "Well that doesn't sound logical. If it's that extreme, why do you wrestle?"

Dan didn't hesitate. "Difficulty overcome is confidence earned."

Billy searched his memory for quotes of the great thinkers of ancient Greece—surely Dan "borrowed" the quote. "Where did you get that saying?" Billy asked.

Dan shrugged and moved on. "I have no idea, but it fits wrestling. Now, here's free advice for surviving the locker room—you need to learn to give as good as you get. You're smart, use humor to fight back. And, for goodness sake, shake hands like a man. Shake my hand again." Billy stuck his hand out and Dan grabbed it. "Keep your wrist solid, and, if there's any movement to the hand-shake, let that come from your elbow. Now, squeeze my hand like you're grabbing the last computer ever sold."

Dan became aware that the lunchroom was watching the tutorial. "What are you looking at? Eat your lunches."

Billy marveled at the response. Heads turned away on command and returned to their meals. He couldn't imagine having that kind of sway over his cat, let alone an entire room full of people.

Dan continued, "I tell you what Butterball—you survive a couple weeks of practice, and you'll have my full endorsement."

Billy smiled. "Well, I'll tell you what Dan, when I receive your full endorsement, I'll help you stay eligible." Mike laughed.

Dan smiled. "That's not bad, Johnson. You might just make it. What is that you're eating? Two candy bars and a coke?"

Billy shrugged. "It's what I always eat."

After lunch, Dan made a beeline for Coach McCreary's office. Dan knocked on the door. "Come in," his coach barked. Hesitantly, Dan stepped into the room. It was always a risk approaching Coach in his office, more times than not you'd find yourself doing free labor. Dan surveyed the stacks of paperwork and envelopes on Coach McCreary's desk. If he loitered too long, it was a good bet Coach would find something for him to do.

"Hey, Daniel, how can I help you?"

As Dan stepped closer to the desk he could see Coach McCreary was busy preparing invitations for the Open tournament that their school would be hosting in a few weeks.

"Well, Coach, I don't want to take up a lot of your time, but you know that kid that Mike Dean convinced to come out for the team?"

Coach McCreary responded while putting stamps on the envelopes, "Yeah, I know the kid, I've got his paperwork right here. From what Mike says, he's going to be quite a project."

Dan continued, "Yeah, that's the guy, and now Mike's got me working on the deal too."

NEARFALL:

Coach was bemused. "What did you guys do, lose a bet?"

Dan provided a courtesy laugh. "Something like that—but anyway, I just had lunch with the kid, and he had two candy bars and a coke. He said it's all he ever eats for lunch. The guy is pretty soft. I was wondering…"

Coach interrupted, "Yeah, I'll take care of it. By the way, I'm glad to see you're feeling better. Keep up the good work, and I'll expect you to win this tournament."

Dan looked at the tournament invitation. "Thanks, Coach, I'll see you at practice." Dan stepped out of the office, took a stride, stopped, exhaled a tortured breath, and turned around. He poked his head back in the office. "Coach, I have study hall this next hour, and well, I don't have any homework, so I guess I could help you with those envelopes."

Coach grinned at the obvious guilt driving Dan's offer. "Nah, I've got this, but I tell you what—if you really don't have anything for study hall. I've got a book I want you to read." Dan looked at the cover of the book that Coach had handed him, "The Legend of Dan Gable."

Matt's grade school was only seven blocks from Mike's school. This was going to be his first wrestling practice, and he really didn't have any idea what to expect. Mike had showed him a few moves goofing around at the house, but Matt had never been to a wrestling practice before. "I hope the coach is cool with me being there."

As he walked past the tightly packed rows of houses his mind drifted to Kimberly. He hadn't yet had an opportunity to duplicate his lip-locking scene with her. They had decided they were going to let the situation cool down before being seen together at lunch

145

and on school grounds. They relegated themselves to the occasional note in class and flirtatious looks on the playground. They had discussed whether to tell their parents about TJ chasing Matt home, and they mulled over the option of telling Mr. Merrill. Matt didn't see the point of telling Mr. Merrill, since he already had sent TJ home for a day and had him cleaning chalkboards and erasers every other day for two weeks.

Instead of the punishment discouraging TJ, it only served as an irritant in a wound—his anger kept festering. Kimberly thought telling their parents would just bring more scrutiny to their "relationship." She convinced Matt that the best thing to do was let TJ run out of steam and get distracted by something else. In the meantime, they could talk on the phone at night and meet on Saturdays. Matt begrudgingly agreed, but all he really wanted to do was kiss her again.

The wrestling manager handed Billy his wrestling shoes and headgear. "Coach wants to see you in his office."

Billy looked confused. "Should I get dressed first?"

The manager glanced over his shoulder as he walking away. "I wouldn't keep him waiting, if I were you."

Billy set his stuff in his locker and headed to the office. Coach McCreary wasn't anything that Billy anticipated him to be. He was expecting a Hulk Hogan type, and instead, there was a medium-sized, normal looking guy, with reddish hair and gray temples. He had seen him in the hallway of school but never knew that he was the wrestling coach or that he taught advanced math.

Billy stepped into his office. Coach had his back to Billy and was looking through some papers. Billy cleared his throat to announce his arrival.

NEARFALL:

"Is the spastic sucking of phlegm considered a greeting where you're from, Mr. Johnson?"

Billy was bewildered. "How did he know it was me? He didn't even turn around."

Billy shoved the thought aside. "No, Sir, I mean, Coach, Sir."

Turning around, Coach handed him three pieces of paper. "It's come to my attention, Johnson, that you eat like a kid in the Willy Wonka chocolate factory. What you have in your hands is a meal plan that you are going to follow if you are going to be on this wrestling team. You will notice the menu is devoid of cakes, cookies, candy, chips, coke and all other soft drinks. This is not a diet. You are permitted to have as much of the food listed as you desire. Suggested meals are outlined. If you have questions or would like to request a deviation from the previously mentioned meal plan, you can submit your request to me in writing explaining the necessity of the change. If I get word that you have gone off this plan, I will come down on you with both feet, and you will do more running than a marathoner. Am I making myself clear?"

Billy quickly looked through the listed foods; he was glad to see that pizza was on the list, although paired with a required vegetable. "Am I allowed any sweets at all?"

Coach nodded, "Yes, you can have plain vanilla ice cream, with fruit and/or chopped nuts."

Billy looked up from the paper. "Is everyone required to eat like this?"

Coach McCreary was matter of fact. "No. There are two other guys that are required. The rest are strenuously encouraged."

Billy had a pained look. "Is that fair, Coach?"

147

Chapter Fifteen

Coach McCreary sat on the edge of his desk. "Your teachers and classmates tell me you're a smart kid, so I'm going to assume that you have a grasp of different forms of governance. This wrestling team you are joining is not a democracy, Son. It is a dictatorship—as you know, the dictator's whim is the law. Do you need help in determining who the dictator is?"

Billy responded quietly, "No, Coach."

Coach stood up and put his hand on Billy's shoulder. "I'm here to help you succeed. Now, because you're new, I'll indulge you. I'm having you eat this way for multiple reasons. I'm teaching you discipline, I'm helping your muscles recover, and I'm getting your adolescent body the nutrients it needs to develop normally. You are joining the team nearly three weeks into practice. There isn't time to bring you along slowly. I need to throw you into the deep end of the pool. This meal plan will help your body repair itself from the training. Do you understand?"

Billy responded, "Thank you, Coach. Although I'm hoping that I won't be that far behind. I checked out a book on basic wrestling from the library. I've familiarized myself with the elementary positioning of wrestling, the rules of wrestling, and the basic objectives of a takedown, escape, nearfall, and pin."

Coach McCreary put his hands on his hips. "How many pages are in this book?"

Billy quickly answered, "258."

"And what page are you on?" Coach McCreary asked.

Billy wanted to make a good impression but felt his answer would fall short. "I'm only on page 51. However, I do feel that I've learned a lot."

NEARFALL:

Coach smiled. "To think, I was concerned. Get out of here, and go get changed for practice."

Billy came into the wrestling room with his head gear already strapped up, which garnered a few snickers from other kids. He took a seat on the mat near Mike. Mike leaned over and whispered to Billy, "Take your headgear off. We don't put that on until we are ready to start wrestling."

Billy whispered back, "I thought that was what we're doing."

Mike nodded, "Yes, but we don't start wrestling immediately."

Billy pulled his headgear off, and took a look around the room. No one was looking at him. He thought he would be a bug under glass that everyone would point to and laugh at. Just as Mike had said, there were kids of all types, body sizes, and backgrounds.

"All right, let's go." Dan started running in a circle around the large and very hot wrestling room. All the other kids piled in behind. Their wrestling shoes pattering on the foam mat like a dysfunctional centipede. For the next twenty minutes Dan led them through a series of calisthenics and wrestling drills. At the end, Coach McCreary blew a whistle. "OK, break. Find a seat." Billy collapsed backward on the mat, splayed out like he was attempting a snow angel. He was drenched in sweat and panting like each breath might be his last.

Mike took a seat next to him. "Billy, sit up."

Billy lifted his head off the mat so that he could look in Mike's direction. "Is it over?"

Mike almost didn't have the heart to tell him. "That was just the warm-up. Now we start practice."

149

CHAPTER 16

Matt sat on the hard wooden bench seats trying to find a comfortable way to watch practice. "Either I'm incredibly small, or this is some sort of sick device to force people to sit up straight." If he tried to lean against the bench behind him, he would fall so far back, he'd practically fall off his own bench. His only other option was to sit like "The Thinker" the entire time, which wasn't especially comfortable either.

Finally, he opted to lie down on the concrete between two rows of benches and prop his head up with his book bag. He softened the "pillow" by balling up his jacket, and setting that on the book bag. "Now all I need is something to drink, and I'm set." He stuck his straw through his drink box and sipped his 100% orange juice. His mother was a taskmaster when it came to juice—there would be no sugary syrups claiming to have some relationship with the tropical fruits of the Caribbean. Matt didn't care. He preferred straight juice anyhow.

As he watched practice, Matt couldn't believe how fast the moves happened once the team started wrestling live. Some of the moves were interesting as the coach demonstrated them, and the guys practiced them, but it wasn't until the live wrestling—when guys were going all out, head to head, that Matt said to himself, "Whoa."

Obviously, not everyone was fun to watch. Some kids were fairly new, so they were like awkward puppies falling over each other. However, the really good guys—they were amazing. Matt discovered a new found respect for Dan. He had no idea he was so awesome. Matt always teased Dan for being a meathead, but Matt could see Dan had real skills. His moves looked just like the coach's did: smooth, fast, and powerful.

Matt had been watching his brother too. Mike wasn't the best on the team, but he was in the top third, which was a considerable improvement over the previous year when he mostly got his butt kicked. "Wow, he's gotten a lot better," Matt thought.

As the practice progressed, Michael would be paired with different opponents. When a couple of them got the best of Mike, he would get so mad, he was practically foaming at the mouth, which Matt found to be hilarious. He took a certain satisfaction in his brother's frustration. It was an odd mix of emotions. He wanted his brother to win, but, at the same time, he enjoyed watching Mike eat some humility.

Matt noticed that practice was winding down, so he laced up his wrestling shoes. They were actually an old pair of Dan's from a few years back that he'd outgrown. Matt started running to get loose and tried to mimic as best he could the stuff that the team had done during their warm-up. He knew that he would need to learn the technique quickly and be nearly as smooth as Mike to handle TJ. The encouraging thing, as he watched practice, was seeing little guys with great moves demolish bigger guys who weren't as skilled. It gave Matt hope.

Chapter Sixteen

Billy was dying, or at least he was convinced he was dying. He could hardly stand let alone try to stop what his opponent was doing to him. If it had been a boxing match, they would have stopped the fight forty minutes earlier. Billy was fatigued beyond reason. No warning or mental preparation could have prepared him for what he was experiencing.

Early in the practice, Billy enjoyed the cerebral exercise of strategy discussion and the learning of technique. But, when it came time for live takedowns, Billy was thrown into a group of whirling little Tasmanian devils. As Billy was taken down repeatedly and his lungs strained for oxygen, his thoughts evoked questions. "Who was this madman, Coach McCreary? Did he formerly torture prisoners for some spy agency? How did the school district allow such an obviously deranged individual loose on children?"

As practice progressed, Billy's brain could no longer assemble such questions, it was focused solely on survival. Flat on his belly, Billy tried to push himself to his hands and knees. As he pushed one arm up and started to come to his knees, his arm was hacked at the elbow by the little rat claw of Speedy Gonzalez. Billy fell face first back to the mat. He quickly pushed back up with his other arm, but, before Billy could get to his knees, Sir Speedy had hacked his elbow and face planted him again. Billy lifted his head just in time to catch a bony forearm right across the mouth. He had read in his book that the move was called a crossface, but, right now, the only thing that it meant to Billy was a bloody lip. The salty taste of his own blood reminded him that he was still alive and fired a thought through his brain, "When will this agony end?"

Unbeknownst to Billy, Coach McCreary had been closely monitoring him. Mike and Dan were correct in their assessment—the kid was excessively pampered and soft, but Coach was encouraged that Billy was hanging in without crying or quitting. For someone brand new, he thought Billy did well during the technique portion of the practice. During breaks, Coach made sure that Billy received extra water, and a few more seconds of breather than the rest of the guys. He knew how to do it without it looking like he was cutting Billy slack. He'd take a moment to show Billy something he was doing wrong, or he'd chew out someone else, but stand in the way of where Billy was supposed to be wrestling.

He made Billy do everything the team did, but paired him with guys that were much smaller and nearly as raw. It was bad luck on Billy's part, but today's practice was going to be one of the hardest the team had had thus far in the season. Middle school was still a place where the emphasis was on fun, but it was his job as a coach to give them the tools and discipline to be successful. He glanced at his watch, and blew his whistle. "Conditioning! Let's go. Let's go. Get moving. You want to be a champion? You've got to pay the price. Perhaps some of you were deluded into thinking that success comes before work. Well, I've got news for you Gentlemen. The only place that occurs is in the dictionary. Buddy carries. Ready…Go!"

Billy clung on as one of the little Tasmanian devils ran back and forth with Billy on his back. "How can this kid do this? I must outweigh him by forty pounds. These wrestlers are superhuman!" As he rested, a sense of dread grimly reminded him that very soon he would be the one doing the running. Billy could scarcely believe that he was expected to run with someone on his back. He was doubtful he could run at all, let alone with a stowaway. His coach bellowed, "Switch." Billy wanted to cry, "Oh dear God please help me."

As Billy staggered along, Matt couldn't help but to watch him. It was like a theatre actor in the last moments of dying, you knew the end was coming but couldn't predict the last gasp. Billy some-

Chapter Sixteen

how completed the task, just as Coach barked out the next command, "Sprints!" The first group took off running; Billy was leaning against the wall to hold himself up. Billy stepped up to the imaginary line. "Next group, Go!" Billy was running for all he was worth when the nausea hit him. Coach immediately recognized that Billy was going to blow. Billy was making a beeline for the sink, and Coach began screaming "Bucket, bucket, bucket!"

The manager kicked the bucket in front of the drinking fountain impeding Billy's progress to the bubbler. Billy heaved directly into the enormous garbage can. It was his last goodbye to his soda and candy bars. Coach waited until the heaving concluded. "All right, Johnson, get a drink and get back out here."

Billy couldn't believe it. "I just blew my guts out, and still he keeps on. This is insanity!"

Matt put his jacket over his mouth to muffle his laughter. He couldn't help it; it was like watching somebody slip on the ice landing flat on their back. Your heart goes out to them, but you can't help laughing. Matt had stopped his warm-up to get out the way of the team's conditioning.

Coach McCreary looked at Matt giggling. He wasn't audible, but he was visible. "Hey, Kid. Get out here. You can run these too."

Matt stopped laughing and still had an "Oh, Oh" look on his face, when Mike gave him a wink. Matt relaxed a little. In Mike's wink he realized that being included was a good thing.

Matt was in Dan's group, and Dan looked at him as the coach was about to blow the whistle. "Matt, I'll give you five bucks if you can beat me."

Matt wasn't sure what he had to do. "Where do we sprint to?"

NEARFALL:

Dan pointed to the end of the room. "Down and back."

Matt smiled and took off like a shot at the sound of the whistle.

Dan caught him on the last couple of strides, and passed him just as they got back to the starting line. "When did you get to be so fast?" Dan asked.

The little scoundrel answered, "Probably when you put five bucks on the line. Double or nothing, I beat you on this next one."

Dan was really tired. He had pushed himself the entire practice. "Nah, I'm pooped."

Matt goaded him by speaking loudly for others to hear, "Come on Superstar. Everybody is watching. Are you really going to let a fourth grader beat you on one little sprint?"

Dan took a deep breath. "All right Punk, double or nothing."

Matt smiled. He couldn't believe Dan fell for it. "Double or nothing—what a moron! I didn't bet anything to begin with, double of nothing is nothing. He's the only one with money on the line." The whistle blew, and Dan burst ahead of the youngster, but Matt changed direction more crisply at the turn, and Dan's legs went to cement. Matt beat him by two strides.

"That's ten bucks you owe me," Matt triumphantly declared.

Dan conceded he'd been beaten. "All right, no problem. Let's see that's… uh… ten cents a week for the next 25 months? You got it Bud. Who do I make the check out to?"

While Matt and Dan were having their little tit for tat, the sprints

Chapter Sixteen

continued. Mike was evaluating his project. Billy was staggering back on each sprint. Mike looked at the clock on the wrestling room wall. Practice would be over soon, Billy was going to make it!

The team completed a few more sprints and then finished with push ups, sit-ups, and pull-ups. Billy needed help with each of the exercises, but he completed them. He lay down on the mat and listened to the blood rushing through his veins. The sound of his heartbeat pounded in his ears. "I'm never doing this again," he thought as he tried to slow his breathing.

In the background, Billy could hear Mike and Dan working with Matt, showing him how to get in a good stance and where to put his hands. A few of Billy's new teammates straggled by to pick up their headgear or work on their takedowns.

"Hey, way to gut it out," said a kid with red wrestling shoes. Another with blue shoes said, "I know how you feel. Don't worry, Dude. It'll get better." Yet another with black and white shoes said, "Hang in there, Man." Billy could only see their shoes as he peered at the world from under the arm draped across his face. Billy was astounded. Yesterday these same guys wouldn't have given Billy the time of day. Now they were encouraging him? Billy thought about something Dan had said at lunch, "Difficulty overcome is confidence earned."

Mrs. Dean was at the gym door to pick the boys up after practice. Mike, Matt, and Dan all piled in. She was driving a rental mini-van until they could pick out a new car.

"How do you like this car, Mrs. Dean?" Dan asked.

Before she could even respond, Matt said, "It's better than the car Dad crashed."

Mike added, "Well, anything is better than what Dad's car looks like now."

Mrs. Dean backed the vehicle up and turned around so she could exit the parking lot. "Well, I like it. I can fit you mongrels in here and still have room for groceries. So, Matthew, how did you like your first day of wrestling practice?"

Matt thought for a moment. "It was boring at first, but there was this one kid that puked. That was pretty cool."

Mike interrupted, "We had a new guy on the team today, and he isn't in shape, so he got sick."

Dan added, "It's Mike's pet project. He's trying to turn a marshmallow into a wrestler."

Mrs. Dean looked in the rear view mirror. "Does this marshmallow have a name, Daniel?"

Dan knew he was being admonished for making fun of his new teammate. "Yeah, his name is Billy Johnson."

Mrs. Dean looked at Matt. "Doesn't your girlfriend have an older brother named Billy?"

Matt squirmed in his seat. He knew he was going to catch flak from Dan if he didn't quickly redirect the conversation. "Mom she's not my girlfriend. Are we getting pizza before we go to the hospital?"

"OHHH, pizza! I'm starving!" Mike chimed in, "Where are we going?"

Mrs. Dean explained, "We are getting take-out, because we're going to have dinner with your father."

Mr. Dean was enjoying the confines of his new hospital room. He

Chapter Sixteen

was out of the intensive care unit and the chest tube had finally been removed giving him a little more mobility. He could sit up in bed and shift a little from side to side. He hoped to be going home in a couple days. Mr. Dean had called Jack Ross, and convinced him to have a courier drop off some materials to the hospital. Mr. Ross was reluctant, but Mr. Dean sold him on the idea that there were only so many episodes of Oprah that he could watch, before he would need counseling.

Mr. Dean glanced at the clock on the wall in front of him. The kids were probably just getting out of wrestling practice. He paged through product descriptions and specifications. Mr. Dean wanted to make sure he knew the products like the back of his hand. When he worked on the factory floor at his previous job, nothing irked him more than a manager trying to tell workers how to do their job without knowing very much about the product. It caused resentment, and now that he was in a management position, he didn't want to be one of those managers.

A knock on the door broke his focus. Mr. Dean looked up to see a short, portly gentleman wearing a baseball cap. He looked to be in his late 40s, maybe early 50s.

"Are you Mr. Dean? The gentleman asked.

Mr. Dean didn't recognize the person standing in the doorway, but was thankful for company just the same. "Yes, I'm Peter Dean. How can I help you?"

The guy seemed a little unsure of himself. "If you're busy, I don't want to disturb."

Mr. Dean set aside the booklets that littered the bed. "Nope, I'm looking for an excuse to quit. I've had my nose in manuals all afternoon. By all means, come on in."

NEARFALL:

Jerry Rusk stepped into the room. "So the doctors say that you're going to be OK?"

Mr. Dean nodded. "Yes, they tell me I'll need to stay in bed for a little while. Unfortunately, they couldn't do anything to make me prettier, but I can't complain."

Jerry smiled. "Well, that's good. I feel a lot better knowing that. I was pretty worried about how you'd come out."

Mr. Dean looked at Jerry curiously. "Were you at the accident?"

Jerry ran his fingers under his ballcap. "Yes sir, I was there." Jerry glanced at the pamphlets near Mr. Dean, "I actually make deliveries for that company that you're researching."

Mr. Dean was flabbergasted. "Really? So what's your impression of the company?"

Mr. Rusk shrugged. "Well, I don't know that much about it. I'm just a truck driver, but I can tell you that the vendors on the other end always speak very highly of the products I deliver."

Mr. Dean was intrigued to hear Jerry's perspective. "That's good to know. So how about the guys at the plant? You must talk to some of them. Do they seem happy with the company?"

Jerry eyed Mr. Dean suspiciously. "Are you an investor or something?"

Mr. Dean laughed. "No, I'm just trying to learn more about the company."

Jerry stuck his hands in his jacket pockets. "Everyone seems to like it fine. I don't hear much grumbling. Occasionally, you might hear somebody wanting more money, but heck, who don't want more money?"

Mr. Dean made a mental note. "I'm sorry I didn't catch your name?"

Jerry cleared his throat. "I'm Jerry Rusk."

They shook hands, and Mr. Dean said, "I was asking, because you and I work for the same company. The morning of the accident I had just been hired."

Jerry rubbed his chin in astonishment. "Well, I'll be... That's amazing. I'm glad I didn't grab that second cup of coffee before I left the factory, otherwise, I wouldn't have seen you go off the road."

Mr. Dean pushed his hand down on the bed in an attempt to sit more upright. "Wow, so you saw me go off the road. Did you see the buck I swerved around?"

Jerry shook his head. "No, I was too far back. I just saw what I thought was a car going off the road, and, when I got to the spot where I thought it happened, there you were at the bottom of the hill."

Mr. Dean looked thoughtful as he tried to piece together what happened. "So you called in the accident?"

Jerry nodded. "Yeah, I called it in and tried to work my way down to you, because I thought there might be kids in the car. But if I had known it was one of my co-workers, I probably would have just stayed in the truck."

Mr. Dean laughed. "Well, that's understandable. You know my

160

kids said something curious. They said when they saw the car on the news it looked like it had burned."

Jerry hesitated, he didn't want to create a fuss or draw attention to himself. "Well, yeah, the car got blazing pretty good after you got out."

Mr. Dean folded his arms in his lap, and looked off in the distance, trying to recall the fire. "The only thing I remember clearly is trying to kick the dash to get my leg out. I vaguely remember smelling gas, but I don't remember any fire."

Jerry continued, "Well, you had pretty much kicked your leg free, but you were still hanging upside down in your seat belt. It was a good thing you had that thing on or you would have been a scrambled egg by the time you reached the bottom of that ravine. You must have flipped that car of yours a good ten times. Well, anyhow, you were a little groggy, so I popped your seat belt off and helped you through the window."

Mr. Dean was wide-eyed listening to the story. "So when did the fire start?"

Jerry ran his hand under his ball cap again and looked at his feet. "Well, it was a little after that, but it was no big deal. We were a ways away from the car at that point. And then the police arrived, followed pretty quickly by those paramedic guys."

Mr. Dean looked at Jerry stunned. "You saved my life."

Jerry shook his head. "Not really. You saved your own life. You somehow had gotten your leg free. I could hear you kicking when I was coming down the hill. You would have gotten yourself out. I just helped a little."

Mr. Dean recognized that Jerry was trying to downplay his role.

161

Chapter Sixteen

"Jerry, you could have stayed in the truck. There was a fire that I don't even remember. I might not have gotten out, and my kids wouldn't have a father. You saved my life. You're a hero. From the bottom of my heart...Thank you."

Jerry couldn't pull his gaze from the floor tile to look at Mr. Dean. All he could muster was a nod of the head and, "You're welcome."

They sat in silence for a few moments, but the quiet was short lived. Matt came bursting through the door. "Dad, we've got pizza!" Jerry moved out of the way as the Dean family tumbled in. Once everyone was in the room, Mr. Dean introduced Jerry, "Honey, Kids, this is Jerry Rusk. He pulled me out of the car before it caught on fire."

They all sat there for a few seconds letting that soak in. Jerry took off his hat. "Nice to meet you, Ma'am. Boys, you've got one tough father there. You should be proud."

Matt spoke first, "Wow, Mister, you saved my dad's life." Matt looked at his mom. "I've never met a hero before. I always imagined them being taller."

Mrs. Dean walked over and gave Jerry a hug. "Thank you. Thank you. Thank you." She kissed him on the cheek. "Is there anything we can do for you?"

Jerry was embarrassed by the attention. "No, Ma'am, it was nothing really. Anybody would have done it. Your husband got himself most of the way out. I just helped with the last little part."

Mike spoke up, "Well, that last part is why my Dad isn't flame broiled. We saw the car. No way could anyone have lived." Mike extended his hand; Jerry gave it a firm shake.

Dan wasn't sure if he should say anything but thought the guy deserved to hear a thank you from everyone. "Mr. Dean is like a second Dad to me. You don't know what he means to all of us— thank you."

Mrs. Dean engaged Jerry again, "Are you sure there isn't something we can do? There is no way for us to repay you. At least let me make you a home cooked meal."

Jerry spied the pizza boxes. "Well, how about a slice of pizza, and we'll call it even?"

Mr. Dean interjected, "Deal! Michael, grab a chair there for Mr. Rusk, and let's dig in."

The boys peppered him with questions while they ate. Jerry, as best he could, tried to answer them all. When they had polished off the food, he bid them all a goodnight and excused himself. He walked down the softly lit hallway with a pride that he had never known. The Deans were a nice family; it comforted him to know that he helped save them from tragedy. Jerry had always thought he could have done better in life if he had chosen a profession other than driving a truck. But, as he reached the elevators, he realized that he was exactly where he was supposed to be.

CHAPTER 17

Much to the surprise of many, including Billy himself, he stuck with wrestling. Nearly four weeks had gone by, and now Billy could honestly say he was starting to get the hang of the routine. The morning after his first practice, Billy couldn't lift his arms to wash his hair, but now he just had a little soreness each morning, nothing major—it was manageable. The person looking back at him in the mirror was starting to surprise him though. His face was thinning; there were apparent cheek bones and a jaw line. His pimples had greatly diminished, and, if he straightened his arm, he could see the bulge of his triceps. It wasn't Arnold Schwarzenegger or anything, but it was definitely there.

The weight was dropping off of him so quickly that he hadn't had time to get new clothes. His belt was cinched to the last notch, and that was now starting to feel loose. He stuck to the food plan Coach McCreary had given him. It wasn't that difficult actually, and he never went hungry. He could still sometimes grab a fast food cheeseburger; he just had to skip the mayo on the bun. He also had to skip the fries and coke and replace them with milk and a salad. It was an adjustment, but it wasn't that drastic, and he never felt deprived.

At school the changes were thrilling. The first week it was just Mike and Dan sitting with Billy, but now there were a half dozen or more kids that regularly dined at Billy's table. They interacted with him. They even sometimes laughed at his wise-cracks—how different life was from a month ago. Back then, Billy could go entire school days without anyone other than his teachers talking to him. Now, he walked down the hall and his teammates gave him a head-bob, "Hey" or "Waz up?" It was such a staggering turn of events, it was almost hard to believe. Billy found it weird to think that withstanding the punishment of wrestling practice and making a few small changes could have such an impact.

His morning routine took a little longer than it used to. Mike had made an appointment for Billy at a salon to get his haircut, and the experience was better than he could have imagined. The girl was college aged, cute, and very friendly—an intoxicating combination for a hormonal young teenage boy. She gabbed away with him as she transformed his tresses and instructed him on how to keep his hair looking its best. Each morning, he attempted to apply the gel, and style his hair the same way she did. It never looked quite as good, but it was much better than what he used to do with his locks—which was nothing. Mike had suggested they wait on the new frames for Billy's glasses. "Let's not go too fast. Otherwise people will accuse you of trying too hard. Let's let you sneak up on them." It seemed like good advice.

Wrestling practice was going a lot better. Billy could now handle those little Tasmanian devils and had been moved up to train with guys that were his size. He could now do four pull-ups unassist-ed at the end of practice, and he was fresh enough to be a partner for Matt as Michael and Dan taught technique after practice. Dan had officially given Billy his blessing, and, surprisingly, asked for some help catching up in math class.

On the downside, Billy had wrestled four matches for his team and gotten pinned in all four. The first time that Billy walked out on the mat in a real match with a real referee with fans in the stands, he thought he going to pass out from the nerves. He survived long enough to get over the butterflies, but was pinned shortly thereafter.

In his last match he was actually winning, but made a rookie mistake. He was trying to stand up off the bottom and reached back with his head down as he came to his knees, leaving himself wide open for a half nelson. Once on his back, Billy was a bit of turtle, and had a hard time getting over to his stomach. He was working on the strength of his neck muscles, so that he'd be better able to bridge up on his head when he was on his back. The idea, as he understood it, was to arch yourself up on your own head—with your opponent still trying to squash you, then quickly drop back down, shoot your arm through the space created, swivel your hips and get back to your stomach, then work back to your feet from there.

It all sounded good in theory, but in application Billy found it a lot tougher to do when your opponent is trying to squeeze you into oblivion. The best option, of course, was not to get put on your back in the first place.

Billy knew he was still the worst guy on the team, but the important fact was that he was ON the team. Wrestling was doing for Billy everything Mike said it would do and more. He hadn't been this happy since before his dad died. In the mirror above his dresser, he gave his look a final once over.

NEARFALL:

Stuck in the corner of the mirror was a 3X5 card. Written on it in permanent marker was the quote that Dan had introduced to him. Billy wanted to look at it every day to remind himself that the effort he was making was moving him in a positive direction. He had modified the saying more to his liking. "Difficulty overcome is RESPECT earned." Billy pushed a couple of hairs to a more desirable location, gave his triceps a flex and laughed at himself. "I guess I can go to school now."

Mr. Dean had set up a command center in his bedroom. He had charts, graphs and stacks of paper everywhere. Mike was hanging a poster board for his dad. On it were the times for each stage of the manufacturing process, along with suggestions from the floor workers on how they could shave time and improve quality. Mr. Dean wanted to look at it as he lay in bed. Next to the poster board was a diagram of the factory floor and snapshots of each step. In his hands Mr. Dean had pictures of the final products and notes from the engineers. If he could just come up with some ways to squeeze time out of the procedures, it would make the company more profitable and the cost savings could be passed on to the customers with lower prices. This would make Mr. Dean's company that much tougher to beat.

"Is this good, Dad?" Mike asked before he applied the tape. Mr. Dean was so absorbed staring at the materials, he didn't answer. Mike waited a few more seconds, but then tried to get his father's attention with increased volume. "Dad!" Mr. Dean looked at Mike on the step ladder, stretched out trying to hold the poster. "Yeah, that looks good, Michael. Thanks for your help on that."

The kids had been troupers during his recuperation. They stepped up and did most of the work around the house that Mr. Dean would normally do—for the most part without complaint. Dan did his part to help out and worked off his punishment splitting two cords of wood for the fireplace.

Chapter Seventeen

Medically, Mr. Dean was doing just fine. He only needed a couple more weeks of bed rest to ensure that his pelvis had healed. The only real concern on his follow-up X-rays was that it looked like Mr. Dean's injured leg would be shorter than the other, once completely healed. This would cause him to walk with a little limp and require a lift in one shoe. Mr. Dean was still optimistic that a lift wouldn't be needed, but after finally seeing the fried remains of his car, he was grateful a limp would be his only burden.

Mike stepped down from the ladder. "Is that it, Dad?"

Mr. Dean took a sip of his coffee. "Yeah, that's great. Thanks."

Mike added softly, "Have a good day."

Mr. Dean looked over his glasses at Mike. "Everything OK, Buddy?"

Michael nodded, "Yeah I'm fine."

Mr. Dean put down what he was working on. "Hey, I want to thank you for all the hard work you've been putting in around here. And I'm sorry that I haven't been able to make it to your wrestling matches. I know you're having a heck of year, only one loss. I hope you know that I really want to be there."

Mike smiled. "Yeah, I know, Dad, I'm just a little tired today."

His Dad returned the smile. "Well, take it easy at practice today. You need to rest up for tomorrow."

Mike gave a little wave as he exited his dad's room. He tried to keep walking, but his feet wouldn't move. "I can't believe I'm going to do this." Mike turned back into his father's bedroom. "Dad?"

NEARFALL:

Mr. Dean looked surprised to see Mike back so soon. "What's up, Bud?"

Mike shifted on his feet; he had worked so hard this season and the big tournament was tomorrow morning. "If you had done something wrong, but something good came out of it, and you didn't do it again and worked really hard, would that make up for the bad thing you did?"

Mr. Dean thought carefully before answering. He knew that there were people that had done great things for the world, after having done some things wrong in their life. However, he could see his son struggling with his conscience. Michael wouldn't be served well by a philosophical discussion. "I think you know the answer to that question."

Mike grimaced at his father's response. He knew what he should do—he just didn't want to lose being able to wrestle in the Open in the process.

Mr. Dean watched the struggle play out on Michael's face. As a father, the range of options for what Mike might have done wrong were frightening. He waited with bated breath for Mike to come clean.

"Dad, a little over a month ago…" Mr. Dean's mind whirled trying to remember what was going on at that time. Mike continued, "I didn't study for a test that I was supposed to, and I was worried about getting a bad grade. I didn't want to get kicked off the wrestling team, so I kind of stole some answers from a kid next to me. I wound up getting one of the best grades in the class."

Mr. Dean nearly exhaled with relief that his son didn't say, "Well, I got drunk, stole a car, and drove it into the lake." But he narrowed his eyes and leaned forward in bed. "You know how I feel

169

about that. So…Michael what do you think your punishment should be?"

Michael's lower lip quivered and tears filled his eyes; he knew the answer, but didn't want to say it.

Mr. Dean lowered his voice. "Well, Michael?"

Mike tried to search for an appropriate punishment that didn't involve wrestling, but couldn't come up with one. "I guess…well I guess…I shouldn't be allowed to wrestle in the Open." Mike sucked back his tears…and his father's heart went out to him. He knew how much this tournament meant to his son, but Mike was young. There would be bigger tournaments. It was important that he learn this lesson now. Mike was still holding out hope that his dad might come up with an alternative punishment, but Mr. Dean gave the answer that Mike didn't want to hear.

"I trust that you'll be having that discussion with your coach today."

Mike clenched his jaw, stared at the carpeting, and nodded his head.

"Did you learn your lesson?" Mr. Dean asked.

Mike looked at his father and wiped away his tears with his flannel shirt. "I sure did."

Mr. Dean continued, "I'm sorry, Son, but I need you to go get your mother for me. I need to talk to her."

Mike left the room, and Mr. Dean leaned back on the pillows propped behind him. He was disappointed in Michael for having cheated, but he was proud that he came clean and accepted his punishment. All of a sudden, shaving a few seconds off stage two on the manufacturing floor didn't seem all that significant.

Mrs. Dean looked at her youngest son as he picked at his breakfast. It wasn't like Matt to not eat. She could tell something was bothering him.

"You nervous about the tournament tomorrow?"

Matt shrugged as he turned his Wheaties over in the bowl. "I guess a little, but it should be OK. I'll have Mike and Dan there to explain how things work."

Mrs. Dean searched for another possible source of angst. "Everything all right with Kimberly?"

Matt took a sip of his orange juice. "Yeah, she's OK."

Mrs. Dean was at a loss. "Did your brother do something?"

Matt suddenly became aware that his mother was on a fishing expedition. He had been answering her questions, but he had been concentrating on his own thoughts, so he hadn't connected the dots. "No, Mike's cool. Everything's fine, Mom."

Mrs. Dean didn't like his "leave me alone" tone. She hooked the back leg of his chair with her foot and pulled Matt's chair away from the table and then hooked the front leg of his chair and swung it toward her.

"You might be able to escape with your life with that attitude when you're sixteen, but not in the 4th grade. Start talking, Pal." Mrs. Dean sat in the chair next to Matt and scooted it so that she'd be facing him. She glanced at her watch. "Hurry up now. I only have ten minutes to solve your problem, save the world, and drive

171

you to school; unfortunately, I still need to iron my cape."

Matt flashed his signature grin hoping he could deflect her. "You're one crazy mom."

Mrs. Dean leaned in. "Crazy like a fox. Now spill it."

Matt sighed; there was no way to throw the blood hound off the trail. "You remember that kid, TJ, who knocked out my tooth and all that? Well, he's still after me, bumping into me in the hall, sending his goons over to harass me on the playground. He chased me home on his bike one day. And he threatened Kimberly and other stuff like that."

Mrs. Dean thought for a moment. "Well, have you told Mr. Merrill?"

Matt shook his head. "It won't do any good. Mr. Merrill has already suspended him once, and he's made TJ do all kinds of work after school. It doesn't faze him. He just gets madder. Kimberly talked me into ignoring him and not letting TJ ever see us together. But last Saturday, he saw us at the bowling alley. He came running after me, and, luckily, Kimberly's friend tripped him, because I was able to get across the street and down the alley before he could see where I had gone. I was hiding behind Mrs. Meyer's wood pile for an hour. I could see him looking for me and yelling for me."

Mrs. Dean groped for solutions. "Well, maybe I should call his parents?"

Matt responded with an emphatic, "No. That will only make things worse. Believe me, he doesn't take punishment normally. He just gets more nuts. He's a big bully, and he needs to be taken care of." Mrs. Dean sat back in her chair. "Is that why you started wrestling?"

Matt nodded. "I figured if I started wrestling, I could take him. So I was sitting here trying to figure out if I'm ready. This tournament will be a test to see if I am."

Mrs. Dean thought she had a brave boy on her hands, but a 4th grader shouldn't be worried about such things. "Matthew, the best way to handle this is to avoid him. He'll move on to other diversions."

Matt looked at his mother. "Yeah, but that will just be someone else to pick on. Should I feel good that he's picking on someone else?"

The implication of passing the buck hung in the air as Mrs. Dean pondered her options. There wasn't another public school to transfer Matt to. Their town didn't have a private school, and, even if it did, the Deans wouldn't be able to afford to send Matt there. The principal was already involved—if this kid was as bad as Matt painted him out to be, then perhaps the police would need to be called.

"Matthew, I know you don't want me to, but I'm going to call Mr. Merrill and update him on the situation. I'm also going to pay a visit to TJ's parents. If that doesn't eliminate the threat, I'll get the police involved. You are in school to learn, not worry about getting beaten up."

Matt was angry. "Mom, please just let it go. I'll handle this guy— I want to handle this guy. Believe me, if I can't take him, Mike will stuff him in a storm drain. I can solve this myself; you can't fix everything for me."

Mom wasn't buying it. "I hear what you're saying Matthew, but resorting to fighting isn't the best option. It's why we have rules and laws. You're a bright boy. Use your head. Beat this guy with your brain. Just keep avoiding him for a little longer, and let me see if Mr. Merrill and I can defuse this. Promise me you won't do anything rash." Matt wouldn't look at her. Mrs. Dean lifted his face up by his chin. "Promise me."

Matt knew his mother wouldn't let him go until he caved. "I promise."

Matt gave his word, but he knew that his mother's phone calls and Mr. Merrill's discipline weren't going to stop a confrontation with TJ. It would only reinforce the probability. He was worried that he didn't have enough training in. "Mike said it would take a couple months of wrestling, I'm only at half that." Matt had been going to practice everyday, and Coach gradually let him do more and more. He seemed to like Matt and the other guys treated him as a mascot of sorts. Matt did all the technique, and conditioning portions of practice. Coach held him out of live wrestling, but Mike would go takedowns with him after practice, and Billy would help out too.

Matt was surprised to learn that Billy knew about Matt's "friendship" with Kimberly. He didn't know how to act at first. "Hi, I'm the guy that's kissing your sister." But Billy was cool, and it wasn't awkward. Dan also stuck around to show Matt extra technique or correct things Matt was doing wrong. When Dan stayed over at the Dean house, he always made Matt lift weights before he went to bed. Matt would go over different techniques in his head and try to remember the little things that really made a difference. Matt could tell he was better. The question was how much better, and would it be enough?

Mrs. Dean was at the stove making eggs for her husband when Mike walked into the kitchen. "Mom, Dad wants to see you."

CHAPTER 18

The morning frost was still heavy on the ground when Matt scraped the ice from the windshield of the Deans' new mini-van. He didn't mind so much, because he got to start the car and listen to the radio while he waited for the others. Matt sat pondering what the rest of the day would bring. He'd never been in a wrestling tournament before. He had no idea what to expect. It was odd to think that he would be the only representative of his household in the competition—although technically Dan could be counted as being on the "home team." Mike's confession had knocked him out of the tournament, which didn't please Coach very much. Mike had been having such a good year; however Coach McCreary understood that character counts.

Matthew toggled the radio dial looking for a good song. An old Elton John song crackled to life, "And you can tell everybody this is your song. It may be quite simple but now that it's done, I hope you don't mind, I hope you don't mind, that I put down in words…How wonderful life is while you're in the world…" Matt listened to the lyrics and thought of Kimberly. If nothing else it took his mind off of the nervousness rumbling around in his stom-

Chapter Eighteen

ach. That is until he remembered that Kimberly was going to be there. "Boy, I hope I don't lay an egg in front of her."

They had weighed in the night before and were paired up by weight and age group. The Deans swung by and picked up Dan on the way to the high school. The tournament was being held at the high school instead of the middle school, because it was the only gym in town that was large enough to hold four complete wrestling mats. The Open was a big event. The age groups started at kindergarten and went all the way through to the ninth grade. The tournament had also gotten a reputation for giving away big trophies. As a result, the competition was fairly fierce with kids coming from all over to be in it. Mike had explained that there would be charts in the hallway showing the pairings by weight class. Matthew would need to find his name on the chart to see who he was wrestling.

The car ride to the high school was much more subdued than normal. Mike was in a foul mood because he desperately wanted to wrestle, and Dan was more quiet than usual, partly because he was annoyed with Mike for coming clean prior to the tournament, and partly because he was focused on taking care of business. Dan had a legit shot to win the tournament, and he wanted that trophy. They pulled up to the gymnasium parking lot, and it was already nearly full.

Matt's eyes got big. "Wow, there's going to be a lot of kids."

Dan looked at Matthew. "You only wrestle them one at a time, Buddy."

Mike added, "Just remember—they put their shoes on the same way you do."

Matt took a breath. "This should be interesting."

NEARFALL:

In contrast to Matt's nerves, Billy was practically euphoric. This was going to be so cool! A huge event of clashing warriors, food, drink, crowds, maybe a few cheerleaders—it was a mini re-creation of the spectacles of ancient Greece, and he, Billy Johnson would be one of the combatants.

Billy cruised into the kitchen where his sister was eating some yogurt and fruit. "You ready to see your brother and your boyfriend do battle against the heathens?"

Kimberly rolled her eyes. "He's not technically my boyfriend. We're not allowed to date, you know that. We just hang out."

Billy laughed, "Oh, really? OK, let me ask a few questions. Are you going to roller rinks, movies, and bowling alleys with any other boy?"

Kimberly softly answered, "No, but we do go in groups."

Billy grabbed a couple of oranges and a banana to take with him to the tournament. "Is his name written repeatedly on your notebook?"

Kimberly's notebook was sitting on the kitchen table next to her, and Billy was still at the other end of the room. She flipped the notebook over so that Billy couldn't see the cover. However, she quickly realized that she had written, "I love Matthew Dean" all over the back too. She sheepishly conceded, "Yes."

Billy closed in on his witness. "One last question, Miss Johnson. Have you kissed him?"

Kimberly's face flashed as pink as the shirt she was wearing and then she huffily puffed at her brother, "I'm not telling you that. That's none of your business!"

Chapter Eighteen

Billy thundered with laughter. His sister's refusal to answer was total confirmation, "You see! He IS your boyfriend!"

Kimberly was completely flustered, and, try as she might, a good comeback escaped her. "Oh, don't be so smug. You're just so, so frustrating to live with."

Billy tossed an orange in the air and caught it behind his back. "Yeah, I know. It's rough for you. I'm not as easy to buffalo as Mom. Come on, let's get going. I can't be late."

Kimberly walked her bowl over to the sink. She was meeting some friends at the tournament from out of town. They had all met during the summer at a girl's camp in Missouri, and Kimberly hadn't seen them in months. She was looking forward to hearing all the gossip from the Camp Kickapoo gang. And, although she didn't want to admit it to her brother, she was really anxious to see Matt wrestle. She was even mildly curious to see how her brother would fare.

She was certainly impressed with the transformation in Billy's mood. Prior to wrestling, he was often quiet and surly. He never had anything good to say about his school. Now he was jabbering excitedly about how he hoped "his buddies" would capture the team championship for the school. She still thought her big brother was a dork, but at least he was a happier dork.

Dan was the first from his team to be out on the mat for warm-ups. He liked getting out early to size up the competition. More accurately, he wanted to let them size him up. Part of the battle was mental, and he wanted his potential opponents to see him focused and confident. Dan had faced a couple of the guys in his weight class earlier in the year. He won, but the matches were fairly close. Dan wanted to prove that those close matches were a fluke. Dan had an undefeated record going into the tournament, and he wanted to keep it that way. Today, he intended to make a statement. He was going to win this tournament, and he was going to win convincingly. He could feel it. He just wanted the tournament to start. There was a guy in his weight class that Dan didn't know who had only lost once, but Dan's attitude was set in stone. "If he comes up against me, he'll be going home with another loss."

Matt stepped out of the locker room just as Billy was arriving.

"Hey Billy, you better hurry up. The tournament is about to start."

Billy was carrying all his gear and his lunch without a gym bag. He was a little harried to say the least. "Yeah, I know, I had all my stuff in a paper bag, and I set it on the floor of the car which apparently was wet. When my Mom dropped us off, the bottom of the sack came apart, and I dumped everything in the parking lot. Besides that, it takes forever to get your girlfriend out of the house."

Matt got a goofy grin on his face. "Girlfriend? She's not my girlfriend."

Billy rolled his eyes. "Yeah, yeah, yeah, I'll see you out there."

Matt walked down the hallway to the gym. He could hear the announcer testing the microphone, "One, two, test, testing one, two..." He stepped into the gym and was overwhelmed. It looked like a chaotic beehive. The bleachers were pulled out and filled with parents, grandparents, and other fans. There were scoring tables at every mat and a half dozen referees standing around drinking coffee and glancing at their watches. The refs all looked like ex-wrestlers, except for one guy who looked like he swallowed a beach ball. His black and white, vertically striped, refer-

179

Chapter Eighteen

ee shirt, barely covered his belly. Matt wondered, "How's that guy going to get down on the mat to see if someone is pinned?" There were people running back and forth to each scoring table with sheets of paper, and there seemed to be a Queen Bee head table that they all reported back to. This head table was the nerve center of the bee hive.

Wrestlers and teams were scattered all over the mats at different stages of warming up. There were fathers helping the really little kids with basic things like stance and how to shoot a double leg takedown. The kindergartners were fun to watch, they were like a bunch of bear cubs wrestling around for the sheer joy of it. They didn't have any concern about doing well in front of the girl they liked.

Matt looked for Kimberly in the stands but didn't see her. He glanced to the bleachers on the other side of the gym, and, while he didn't spot Kimberly, he did see Dan waving like a maniac to get Matt's attention. Dan was leading the team through stretching.

Matthew cut across the mats and dodged the wrestlers drilling moves. Every team had a different color warm-up or sweatsuit. Matt looked at his old Green Bay Packer sweatshirt and wished he had an authentic team warm-up. Some of them were pretty cool looking. Matt wasn't "officially" on any team which meant he was wrestling "unattached." However, the guys that he had been working out with for the last month welcomed him as one of their own.

Dan immediately corralled Matt and started rough housing with him. He grabbed the back of Matt's neck and gave it a little pull, forcing Matt to take a step forward. Dan caught Matt's foot as he stepped, picked it up by the heel, and dumped Matt on his butt.

"That's called an ankle pick."

NEARFALL:

Matt was a little mortified that he had fallen over so easily. He would've liked to look a little more cool in front of Kimberly and her friends. "Hopefully, they're not in the gym yet," he thought.

Dan was sitting on the mat and leaned back on his hands. "Have you seen Billy?"

Matt nodded, "Yeah, he's in the locker room getting dressed. Where's Mike?"

Dan yawned. "He's out looking at the charts seeing who you wrestle first, and, no doubt, looking at his weight class with despair. He would have done really well here today." Dan looked at Matt who seemed to have his head in the clouds. "Hey, you nervous?"

Matt picked at the shoelace on his wrestling shoe and pulled up the tongue. "I don't know. A little I guess. I kind of wish Billy's sister hadn't shown up. What if I bomb?"

Before Dan had a chance to answer, Billy came bounding across the mat and sat down next to Dan. He said hello to everyone and was as happy as a lark.

"How about you, Johnson, are you nervous?" Dan asked.

Billy was effusive, "Heck, no, this is awesome. What we're doing here dates back to ancient Greece when wrestling tournaments were fought to the death. We're living out a heritage that dates back thousands of years."

Dan pointed to Billy. "Now, you see Matt, he's got the right frame of mind. Just go out and battle and give the crowd a show. The rest will take care of itself. By the way, Johnson, for the record, I tuned out as soon as you said the word ancient—but I respect your enthusiasm."

Chapter Eighteen

Michael was walking into the gym as the announcer took to the mic, "WRESTLERS clear the mats!" The crowd let out a cheer as the teams headed into the stands and locker rooms to await their weight classes. The guys who had matches first started getting their last warm-up in on the small mats in the back hallway. Mike caught up with Matthew as he was headed into the stands near where Mrs. Dean was sitting.

"Hey, Matthew, your age group is going to be on Wrestling Mat Two through these early rounds."

Matthew looked around at the gym. "How do you tell which one is Mat Two?"

Mike pointed to the roman numerals taped on the corner of the mats. "It's also on top of the score board. Do you see it?"

Matthew looked and acknowledged that he did.

Mike was talking loud because the announcer was calling wrestler pairings to the mats to start the tournament. "If you forget, just remember you're on the black mat for these early rounds. All you need to do is watch that mat and listen for your name. If you're the next up, they'll tell you that you're 'on deck.' If you're one behind that, you're 'in the hole.' Got it?"

Matt leaned over so Mike could hear him. "Did you see who I wrestle first?"

Mike nodded, "Yeah, it's some kid named Joe Bye. I'm not sure where he's from, but I saw him warming up in the hall. He looked pretty tough. You better be ready."

Matt felt his throat tighten. He was hoping for a guy that was new, like himself.

Mrs. Dean was taken aback. "I can't believe you are going to do that to your own brother. This is his first tournament, Michael."

Mike protested, "But Mom, it only works the first tournament. The new guys are wise to it after that."

Matt looked thoroughly confused. Mrs. Dean leaned forward. "You don't have a match this first round. You have a bye because there are an uneven number of guys in your weight class."

Matt asked, "How does that happen?"

Mrs. Dean continued, "It's just the luck of the draw. Congratulations. You've advanced to the next round. Your brother was just messing with you."

Matt threw his headgear at Mike who was holding his stomach with laughter. "Ah, you should have seen your face! Priceless!"

Mrs. Dean interrupted, "You two should go down and sit with your team. I've got some lunches packed in the cooler, if you get hungry."

Kimberly and her girlfriends settled into their seats. Tara, the oldest of the girls by two years, was cute, spunky, and absolutely googly-eyed at the prospects. "Have you ever seen so many boys with muscles in one place?" Kimberly tossed her hair with indifference. "Muscles aren't everything." Heather, who shared a room with Kimberly at camp and was the same age, giggled, "Yeah, that might be true, but they sure are fun to look at." Rounding out the group was Lisa; she was pretty and just a year older with blond hair. "Which one is your brother, Kimster?"

Kimster was the nickname Kimberly had picked up at camp. She didn't particularly like it, but it was only used within the confines of the Kickapoo gang. Kimberly scanned the gym and spotted him warming up. "He's right over there bouncing up and down by Mat Three. He's in the blue sweatsuit." All the girls looked at Billy.

"Oh, he's cute!" exclaimed Lisa.

Tara asked, "Does he have a girlfriend?"

Kimberly wrinkled her nose like she had just smelled dog poop.

Heather chimed in, "You know who he looks like? He looks a little like Keanu Reeves, only bulkier."

Kimberly waved her arms in front of friends. "Hello? Do you guys need glasses? Have you taken a stupid pill? My brother is a dork. He's a nice guy, and I love him to death, but he is definitely NOT cute!"

All three girls looked at Kimberly like she was nuts. Tara spoke first, "You just think that, because he's your brother."

Kimberly emphatically shook her head. "No, I'm telling you, my brother is the biggest geek on the planet."

The girls just ignored her. "How long has he been wrestling?" Lisa asked.

Kimberly couldn't believe this was happening. "Out of all the guys that were at this event, why would they care two cents about Billy?" She reluctantly answered Lisa, "I don't know, maybe a month or so."

The girls came from a town that was really big in wrestling, so they knew not to expect much, "Well, this will be good experience for him," Heather offered and then posed the next question. "Kimster, where's your man?"

NEARFALL:

Kimberly looked around the gym and pointed directly across the gym. "You see that team in blue just right of the aisle? He's the third guy in, on the second row. He's wearing a gray sweatshirt."

All three of the girls looked at Kimberly like, "Dang Girl! He's smoking."

Kimberly blushed, "Yeah, he's pretty cute."

Billy didn't have high expectations. He was just happy to be in the tournament. His goal was to wrestle well and not get pinned. As he warmed up, he took it all in. In his imagination, he was transported back to the arenas of the first Olympiad in Athens.

Billy, probably more than anyone in the gym, understood the proud legacy of wrestling and its lofty place in history. He was honored to carry on that tradition, and it made his body surge with adrenaline. Dan was also warming up for his match. He'd be going to battle soon after Billy. He came over to make sure Billy knew that he was on deck. "You know you're next, right?" Billy nodded that he did.

He looked at the clock; there was less than a minute in the match. He took off his warm-up sweats and put on his headgear. Dan walked by again and wished him good luck. All of a sudden little butterflies hit Billy, but he smirked at their arrival. "I wonder if the first Olympians felt this same sensation?" He took a deep breath.

The match ended, and Coach McCreary walked up to Billy. "You ready to go?"

Billy responded, "Yes, Coach," and took a sip of water from the manager.
Coaches were allowed to coach from the mat. There were chairs

185

Chapter Eighteen

on two opposite corners of the mat where each coach would sit. Billy put his sweats behind Coach McCreary's chair and started to run out on the mat, but Coach McCreary grabbed his arm. "Keep your head up, stay in good position, and wrestle smart. OK, go get him."

Billy ran out to the center of the mat where the ref was standing with the bout sheet. "Billy Johnson, you're green. Heath Parsons, you're red. Billy grabbed the green leg band and put it around his ankle. He stepped to the center, toeing the line. Heath Parsons did the same. They shook hands. Billy dropped into a wrestling stance. The ref looked at the score table. "Timer ready? OK, Gentleman, here we go."

He blew the whistle, and the two opponents collided. Billy tried an arm drag, but Heath pulled his arm back before Billy could get a good grip. Heath faked grabbing Billy's head and shot in on a single leg takedown. Billy sprawled his legs back, but Heath got an angle and switched off to double leg takedown. Billy fell to his side. Coach McCreary was yelling, "Get to your base. Get to your base." Billy got to his knees and attempted to stand up, only to have his opponent switch off to a tight-waist-far-ankle and drive him back to the mat. Billy didn't escape the rest of the period, but he also didn't get turned to his back.

The second period nearly mirrored the first, except that Billy gave up a point for an escape, as his opponent got away from him. He again got taken down on a single, switched off to a double leg takedown, and was ridden out for the remainder of the period. Heading into the third and final period, Billy was losing five to zero. Each takedown was two points and the escape his opponent scored was one point.

Billy started the third period kicking himself. He could see opportunities, but he didn't react fast enough to take advantage. The ref's whistle blew, and final period was underway. Billy again tried to stand up, but was slammed face first back to the mat. Matthew cringed at the sound of Billy's face slamming against the mat.

Mike turned to his brother. "Hey, at least he's hanging in there. He's not getting pinned." Kimberly actually covered her eyes; even if she thought Billy was a dork, he was her brother, and she couldn't bear to see Billy get hurt. Her friends were watching and they were enthusiastically giving her the play by play.

Billy's opponent, Heath, seemed determined to try to pin Billy instead of just coasting to victory. He kept coming out front trying to drive a half-nelson, but each time Billy reached up, peeled it off, and looked away from the pressure, just as he was taught. Heath was even trying to crank Billy over when Billy was on his hands and knees.

Billy's mind was frantic for a solution. He remembered in his reading something about hitting a side roll if your opponent was trying to go for the kill, and driving too hard. Usually, when an opponent would do this, they would have a tight waist ride on. Billy could feel Heath's arm cinched taut—the tight waist was definitely being applied. Billy tried to picture the diagram from the wrestling book. "Let's see, if I hook the elbow and hip down to the side using my opponent's momentum, he should flip right over the top and go flat to his back, I think. I hope." Billy noticed that Heath was driving hard. Billy hooked the elbow, closed his eyes, and hipped down as hard as he could. When he opened his eyes, to his utter amazement, he was looking into the panic stricken face of his opponent.

Coach McCreary was screaming, "Reverse your half! Get perpendicular! SQUEEZE!" Mike, Matthew, and the rest of their teammates leapt to their feet. "SQUEEZE!" Kimberly spread her fingers peering out between them, her friends were going nuts! Dan was at the edge of the mat. "Stick him!"

Billy clamped down for all he was worth. The seconds ticked by, and he could hear the ref counting out nearfall points. His opponent was struggling to keep his shoulder blade from touching the mat. Billy saw the ref's hand go in the air. The ref slapped the mat, "Fall!" Billy jumped up in the air and pumped his fists. His teammates went crazy! He shook hands with the vanquished Heath, and the ref raised Billy's hand. He was absolutely exhilarated! He just couldn't believe it.

He had started to walk toward Coach McCreary, when the ref interrupted his departure from the mat. "Son, you need to sign your bout sheet at the scorer's table."

Billy looked back at the ref with a broad, toothy grin. "Sorry, Sir, I've never won before."

Billy signed the bout sheet and headed over to Coach McCreary. "Does it feel pretty good to get that first win out of the way?"

Billy grabbed his warm-ups from his coach. "I think it's the single greatest moment of my life!"

Coach McCreary chuckled, "Well, you're young, Son. You'll have a lot more. Good job."

Billy went back over to the bleachers to sit with his teammates, while he put his warm-up sweats back on. The back slaps and congratulations were plentiful and appreciated. Billy felt like a million bucks. He looked back at Mike a couple of rows behind him, nodded his head, and gave Mike a thumbs up. Mike acknowledged Billy's gesture with a nod of his own and mouthed the words "You're welcome."

NEARFALL:

Dan's match was practically over before it started. The whistle blew and Dan's opponent charged directly into him. Dan redirected him with a head snap and quick outside single that missed. Dan came back to his stance and the guy again charged him. This time Dan hit a quick hip toss, and, when his opponent finally landed, Dan was there to wrap him up tighter than a tube sock on a five hundred pound postal worker. It was a pin in twenty seconds. Dan signed his bout sheet, grabbed his gear, and jogged back to the bleachers. He took a seat next to Mike. Mike didn't even look at him. "Show off." Dan didn't look at Mike either. "I'm pacing myself."

After watching the first round, Matthew felt a little more comfortable with his surroundings. He began to make sense of it all. As his weight class approached, he headed down to warm up. Michael came down from the bleachers to stand with Matt; if he couldn't wrestle, perhaps he could be of some help to his brother. Matt was still nervous, and he couldn't shake it.

"Hey Mike, any advice?"

Mike kept it simple. "Just have fun, set up your shots, and go."

Matt spotted Kimberly in the stands and smiled. "Just keep it fun," he repeated to himself, "Just keep it fun."

Now that his match was upon him, everything seemed to be happening so quickly. It was a blur. Before he knew it he had his sweatshirt off, his headgear on and he was out on the mat. The ref blew the whistle, and Matt took a quick shot, but was countered. Coach McCreary joined Michael in the corner to help instruct Matthew. "Your brother is quick." Mike nodded in agreement.

Matt was darting in and out with half shots trying to get an opening. Dan came over to tell let his coach know that he was on deck on another mat. Coach McCreary looked over his shoulder. "Already?"

Dan shrugged, "I guess they changed the order this round." Dan crouched down by the chairs to watch a little of Matt's match. Matthew grabbed his opponent's head at the back of the neck, gave it a little snap forward and when his opponent took a step to maintain his balance, Matthew dropped down, caught the guy's heel with his hand, quickly changed direction, and dumped his opponent right on his butt—a textbook ankle pick. Dan backhanded Mike on the shoulder. "I just showed him that for the first time this morning! He didn't even practice it. Wow, that's cool!" Dan jogged back over to his mat because his match was about to start.

The period ended with Matt winning two to zero, but he was sucking wind. Wrestling in real match conditions was exhausting. Coach McCreary gave Matthew a couple of words of encouragement, and then walked over to Dan's match to coach him. Michael motioned for Matt to put his hands on his head and take deep breaths.

Matthew was starting on the bottom in the second period. The ref called Matt to the center to get in position. "Wrestlers set?" He blew the whistle to start the action. Matthew immediately tried to hit a switch, but his opponent stepped across and thwarted the effort. Matt struggled to get to his feet, but the other guy was hanging tough.

Kimberly just couldn't bring herself to yell. She was too nervous watching Matt. Her friends however, were not having any such restraint. "Come on Matt, stand up!"

Mrs. Dean tried to be very contained, but she leaned and moved with the action on the mat as if her body English would help Matthew.

NEARFALL:

Mike was yelling, "Peel the hands, get hand control, and stand up!" Matthew glanced at the clock--twenty two seconds left in the period. He finally made it to his feet and used both hands to attack his opponent's grip. He focused on the thumb peeling it down to weaken the grasp. It loosened just enough for Matt get his hip out. Once that was accomplished, he was able to spin away for a one point escape.

However, the effort took its toll—Matthew was completely gassed. He leaned heavily on his opponent—too heavily, his adversary hit a duck under and scored a takedown with five seconds left in the period.

Matt was still winning, but his body language was that of someone who was getting beat. Mike yelled, "OK, shake it off. One period left, suck it up! You're up three to two, be smart. You've got this."

Dan came and sat down in the chair next to Mike. "You're done?" Mike asked.

Dan shrugged, "I wanted to see the rest of this match."

Mike shook his head in reprimand. "Well, you could be more diplomatic and let your victims score a couple points first."

Dan ignored him. He was too busy cheering on Matthew who had just caught a lucky break when his overly anxious foe false started twice, giving Matt a point—and, most significantly, a breather.

Matt now had a four to two lead. Michael was sweating bullets; he leaned over to Dan. "I think I get more worked up coaching than I do when I'm wrestling." The whistle blew, and Matt broke his challenger down. All Matthew had to do was keep his opponent from escaping, and he'd win. Matt strained to hang on. He shifted from one side to the other, chopping the arm that his rival braced himself on, and then drove him to his stomach.

As the final period wore on, Matt kept stealing glances at the clock, which, unfortunately, did not escape the ref's attention. He warned Matthew for stalling. Another stalling warning and Matt's opponent would be awarded a point. Matt tried to come out front and make it appear that he was going for a pin, but it gave his opponent some space, and he made it to his feet. Matt just didn't have the strength to hold on, and his opponent pulled away. With the escape, Matt was clinging to a narrow one point lead.

Mike yelled out the time, "Twenty seconds left!"

Dan was screaming "Circle, circle, keep moving!"

Matt allowed himself to be maneuvered toward the boundary at the edge of the mat. His opponent took a desperate shot as the clock ticked down to seven seconds. Matthew defended the shot, but being so close to the edge of the mat, he figured he'd let the momentum carry them out of bounds. Just as Matthew relaxed, his opponent drove his shoulder into Mat's shin. The pain dumped Matt right on his backside. As time expired, the ref awarded two points for a takedown.

Matthew started to protest, but noticed that his opponent had managed to keep his toes inside the line and his knees never touched out of bounds. Like a wide receiver getting both feet down on the sideline when making a catch, Matt's adversary pulled off the same tightrope stunt; Matt lost 5-4.

Mike put his arm around his brother as he was coming off the mat. "Hey, not bad for your first ever match—the lesson is, never to relax on the edge of the mat."

NEARFALL:

Dan tried to cheer Matthew up. "I can't believe you hit that ankle pick—that was awesome."

Matt listened to both of them, but all he really wanted was water and air. He found a blank area on the gym floor on the far side of the bleachers and thankfully lay down. He put his sweatshirt over his eyes to block the lights from overhead. "Holy cow, I've got to get in better shape."

Billy got killed in his next match, dropping him into the consolation bracket. But he scored an 8-7 victory the following round. It was a sloppy match, but a win, nonetheless. He finished the day losing 6-3 in the consolation finals and placed sixth in the tournament, a result far exceeding his expectations. It was like a dream come true.

Matt's loss also dropped him into the consolation bracket. He rebounded strongly with two consecutive victories, pinning his opponent in the consolation finals and picking up fifth place. He felt good about the day and was glad he finished strong.

Dan hardly broke a sweat the entire tournament. He finished with four pins, the last of which didn't come until the end of the second period. Mike looked disgusted as Dan came off the mat. "What happened? I had money on him going down in the first round. Some kind of friend you turned out to be." It was Mike's way of saying, "Wow, that was impressive," while still giving his buddy a hard time.

Dan, of course, won the tournament and picked up the most valuable wrestler award as a bonus. He was even interviewed by the great sports reporter, Mike Chapman. Matthew overheard Mr. Chapman say to Coach McCreary, "This Dan Morgan kid looks like he could be something special."

Chapter Eighteen

Matt parroted the quote to his mom and Michael. Mrs. Dean explained that it was a HUGE compliment, because Mike Chapman had been covering wrestling for years. She added, "Too bad his father doesn't know how special Dan is." Dan's father didn't even so much as make an appearance at the tournament.

The team wound up in third place, which was another stab of guilt to Michael's stomach. Had Mike wrestled, he probably would have scored enough points to push the team into first or second place. Mike watched his friends pose with the third place trophy. The acid taste of disappointment that comes from having no one to blame but yourself pervaded his world. "Next year, I'm winning this tournament."

CHAPTER 19

Matt looked in the mirror. Wrestling in live matches, against real opponents took on a different level of intensity, and it showed up on Matt's face. He had a bruise/mat burn combination on his forehead, his lip was split, and on one eye it looked like he had mascara from the black eye. Matt took a last look at his appearance and stepped into the hallway. His brother and Dan were talking to Mrs. Dean and some other parents. Kimberly was standing with her girlfriends and motioned for Matt to come over. She was as pretty as ever, and her smile still made his heart skip a beat.

As Matt approached the group, they all congratulated him on wrestling well, and Matt graciously thanked them. Kimberly was careful not to show too much affection. She didn't want to lend credibility to her brother's "boyfriend" accusation.

"Hey, Matt, the girls and I are going to walk to Sammy's Pizza. Do you think your Mom will let you walk with us?"

Matt didn't think it would be a problem. "Let me ask. I'll be right back."

Chapter Nineteen

As Matt turned away, Tara asked, "Hey Kimster, will you ask your brother to come with us?"

Kim tried to beg off, "Oh, he eats a pretty strict diet now. I don't think he'd want to go; besides I don't know where he is. He might be in the showers."

Tara pleaded, "Come on, Kimster—for me?"

Billy walked out the gym doors and spied Michael and Dan. "Hey, Coach wants everybody in the gym to finish rolling up the mats." Billy looked specifically at Dan. "Hey, Dan Morgan, what, you win a trophy, and you're above manual labor? I don't know, Bud. I think you're getting soft in the head. I've seen sticks of room temperature butter with more mental toughness."

Michael laughed, "Oh, Dude, he got you good!"

Dan calmly turned to Mike. "Could you hold this please?"

He handed Mike the trophy. Dan locked his gaze in Billy's direction like a predator looking at his prey. Dan pounced, and Billy took off running—laughing the entire way. Billy used the mats, his teammates, his coach, and anything else he could run behind to elude Dan. "Ah, come on, Dan, I was just trying to keep you humble. OK, wait. I'm sorry...let's just sit down... and do some algebra together, you big Neanderthal."

Dan laughed and gave chase even harder, finally catching Billy and tackling him on the mat. Coach McCreary was getting a hoot out of their antics, but now it was time to call it a day. "All right, Guys, that's enough. Let's get this last mat rolled up. We need to clear the gym."

Matt had waited patiently for his mother's attention. She finally wound up her conversation. "Mom, would it be OK if I walk with Kimberly and her friends to Sammy's."

Mrs. Dean looked over the group. They seemed to be pretty good kids. "All right, but be careful. I'll tell you what. I'll meet you there in an hour to pay for the pizza. I'm going to run home quickly and check on your father."

"Here Mom, give him this. That way I won't lose it." Matt handed her his fifth place ribbon.

Mrs. Dean looked at it and tussled Matt's hair. "You did really well today, Kiddo. I'm proud of you."

"Ah, Mom, now I've got to go comb it again." Matt flashed his bread and butter grin. "You know it takes effort to look this good."

Mrs. Dean sighed, "Oh, brother! You're something else. I'll see you at Sammy's."

Matt walked back to Kim and her group. "Yeah, I can go. My mom is going to meet us there and spring for the pizza."

Kimberly looked at the imploring faces of Tara, Lisa, and Heather. "OK, cool. Umm, do you know what any of the other guys are doing? Specifically, my brother?"

Matt shrugged, "I don't know what your brother's doing, but a bunch of the guys are going to Sammy's."

Kimberly looked at Tara again and her sorrowful expression. "Oh, for goodness sakes! I'll go ask him." She looked at Matt. "Wait here, I need to go talk to my brother."

Kimberly walked into the gym, and her brother was helping load the mats on the carrier. She sauntered up beside him. "Hey, Billy, you don't want to go with me to eat some really unhealthy, greasy pizza do you? A couple of the girls thought you might like to go, but I told them you wouldn't want to hang out with gradeschoolers... right?"

Kimberly was really stretching, because Tara was only a year younger than Billy. Billy looked at his teammates near him who had overheard Kimberly's question. "Uh, no. I think I'll just head home. I'm pretty sore. I think I'll just watch a movie or something. Thanks, though." Kimberly smiled. "Yeah, that's what I thought you'd say. OK, I'll see you later. Good job today."

Billy pulled the strap tight on the mat. "Thanks, Kim. I'll see you later." Billy turned to his teammates who were still looking at him. "That's my sister. Just be quiet."

Things were winding up. What had been noisy and chaotic was quickly returning to a big empty gym. The only evidence of the tournament pageantry was litter collecting in front of the janitor's push broom. Mrs. Dean pulled Mike aside. "Do you think you could follow your brother, but stay far enough back so that he didn't know you were there?"

Mike furrowed his brow. "You want me to spy on my brother?"

Mrs. Dean shook her head. "No, I'm just concerned. He's got this guy that's been threatening him at school and in general just being a real bad seed. I called the school yesterday and the boy's parents. Matt seems to think this kid is not right in the head, so I was just wondering if you and Dan could keep an eye on Matt for a couple weeks."

Mike was seething. "This is that TJ kid, right?"

Mrs. Dean could sense the thoughts boiling in her son's brain.

NEARFALL:

"Just keep on eye on him. Don't go off half cocked and get yourself in trouble. If you see this TJ starting anything, just call me or the police. You understand?"

Mike begrudgingly agreed. "Yeah, all right. Dan and I will follow them to Sammy's, but I still think my way would be better."

Billy cut through some yards trying to get home as quickly as possible. There were a few fences and hedges that had to be navigated, but Billy was certainly trying to apply the principle that the shortest distance between two points is a straight line. It was cold out, and he was hungry. Once he got home, he still needed to cook the chicken, steam some broccoli, melt the cheese...all that was going to take a little time. Plus, if he got home soon enough, he might catch the beginning of the Star Trek marathon.

Billy looked up from his thoughts—his straight line path was blocked by a big Victorian home. He contemplated which way to go around it. He glanced down the side street. His stomach was really grumbling. "Pizza wouldn't be horrible. I ate really well during the day. Plus, I could order a side salad and a milk." Billy figured if he cut down the side street and followed that toward the big Catholic Church, he'd probably catch up to his sister. He pondered Kimberly's invite. "A couple of those girls looked older than Kim, and THEY asked her to ask me...wait just a minute...when was the last time a girl of any age asked me to do anything? What was I thinking?—Of course I'll go have pizza with them." Billy turned abruptly to the right and picked up the pace.

Mike and Dan were hanging back trying not to be noticed by Matt. They were maybe two to three blocks behind Matt's gaggle of girls. Dan was mildly annoyed. "Tell me again why we're playing wet nurse to your brother?"

Chapter Nineteen

Mike exhaled emphatically. "I don't know. It seems like a waste of time to me."

Dan and Mike were of the same mindset. "Why don't I go have a 'conversation' with this TJ kid? Your Mom said you shouldn't do it. She didn't say anything about me. I'm expendable."

Mike got excited. "Hey, you know what? That's a great idea! I think that would work!"

Dan looked hurt. "Are you saying I'm expendable?"

Mike was practically bouncing like Tigger. "That's exactly what I'm saying! If you catch an accidental baseball bat to the head, who'd miss ya?"

Dan pushed him in the chest. "Shut up!"

When Dan shoved him, Mike noticed that Dan was missing something. "Hey, where's your trophy?"

Dan got a look of horror on his face, "Oh, man, you've got to be kidding? I left it with you."

Mike protested, "I left it on the bleachers when we finished up in the gym, I thought you saw it there."

Dan was beside himself. "I can't believe you. You get yourself booted from the tournament, so you've got to steal the trophy I earned? Man, that's low."

Mike stopped and looked at Dan, he couldn't even fathom that Dan would say such a thing. Nothing was said for a few seconds. It felt for a moment that things might get heated. Mike finally realized that Dan was kidding. "Ah, you suck."

NEARFALL:

Mike punched Dan in the shoulder, Dan laughed. "You are so gullible. By the way, I'm building condos on the floor of Lake Superior, would you like to buy a couple?"

Mike looked curious. "Really? What's the square footage? So, seriously, where's the trophy?"

Dan threw a rock down the sidewalk, "Well, I knew I couldn't bring it home, because my old man would just use it for an ashtray, or a door stop. So, I asked Coach if he could keep it in his office. So, that's where it is. If you buy a ticket you can go and look at it from time to time."

Mike laughed. "Oh man, I can see you're going to be tough to live with for a couple weeks."

Dan strained to see in the darkness. "Can you still see your brother?"

Kimberly was holding onto Matt's arm as they walked. "You did really good today. I was proud of you." Matt didn't know how to accept the compliment. "I should have beaten that first guy." Matt was learning what many wrestlers come to learn—you remember the details of the losses better than the details of the victories. And Kimberly was learning that all guys need an ego boost from their gal from time to time. "Ah, come on, it was your first tournament. I thought you did great." She looked up and gave him a kiss on the cheek. "Is that better?" Matt blushed, "Yeah, actually."

Kimberly's friend Heather screamed at the top of her lungs, "LOOK OUT!"

Matt turned to see TJ only a few feet away and running full blast. Matt pushed Kimberly out of the way just as TJ barreled into his midsection. The impact knocked Matt flat, and the back of his head hit the gravel in the alley. Matt was stunned and tried to scramble off his back as TJ's blows rained down on him. TJ was screaming, "You think you can get me suspended and have Mommy fix this for you!"

Kimberly was screaming at TJ as she saw a punch drive Matt's head backward. "TJ, leave him alone! Get off of him!"

TJ looked back at Kimberly. "Shut up! I'll deal with you next!" Heather and Tara screamed for help. Lisa was too shocked to do anything.

Mike and Dan continued walking, but lengthened their stride, because they couldn't see Matt. "Looks like they went down the alley behind Burger King," Dan offered. Mike thought about stopping at Burger King, but decided he could wait until pizza...besides, he had come up with another option. "Hey that means they're going right behind the Mill House. You can finally pay me those Toaster Tarts you..."

Dan interrupted him, "Shush, you hear that?" Mike cocked his head to listen. He heard it too. In a flash he was in a full sprint.

Matt had been absorbing some punishment, but he was finally able to get one knee under himself and braced off on his hand. He saw an opening and swung his head to the outside of TJ's hip. He planted his outside leg, reached across to TJ's knee, and drove for all he was worth. Matt pulled on TJ's knee and it collapsed as Matt pushed TJ's weight across it. TJ fell to his side, and suddenly Matt was on top of him. Matt anchored his leg around TJ's with a grapevine and slammed down his left forearm on the back of TJ's neck. With his right hand, he came under TJ's right arm. Matt locked his hand on his own forearm, grinding TJ's face into the rocks.

Once locked, Matt cranked for all he was worth. TJ screamed

out in pain as his face raked across the gravel, and his right elbow was relocated behind his neck inching steadily closer to the left side of his head. TJ tried to get off his stomach, but his body was pinned tightly to the ground and he couldn't move. The pain was excruciating. Matt knew he had him dead to rights and could dislocate his shoulder, but he remembered his mother's words and refrained. "TJ, do you give up?"

TJ screamed, "Not a chance, Worm!"

Matt gritted his teeth and cranked harder. TJ cried out, "All right, All right. I give up!"

It went against Matt's better thinking to do anything short of hospitalizing him. He gave one more crank for emphasis. "It's over, TJ, you hear me? You are never going to bother Kimberly or me ever again. Right?"

Matt gave another crank. "Yes! Yes! I quit. Yes!"

Matt gathered his thoughts. "OK, TJ, here's how it's going work, I'm going to release you and stand up. You're going to get up and walk away. Understand?"

TJ whined like a little girl, "You're hurting me Matt. Let me go."

Matt released his lock, untwined his leg and pushed off. TJ laid on the ground for several seconds, and Matt walked toward Kimberly and the other girls.

Kimberly was standing with her mouth open. "Holy mackerel, how did you do that?"

Matt shrugged, "Wrestling."

Chapter Nineteen

As Matt stepped into the light of the streetlamp above, her face changed to concern. "Matt, you're bleeding." Matt was surprised. "I am? Where?" Matt touched his neck, he felt the wet blood running down his skin. "I must have hit my head on a rock." Matt touched the hair on the back of his head. It was wet with blood. "Kimberly, look to see how bad this is." Matt bent down so she could get a better look.

Kimberly thought she might vomit there was so much blood. Matt tried to encourage her. "It probably just looks worse than it is. I've had stitches in my head before, and the doc said the head and face bleed a lot."

She was trying to separate the blood soaked hairs when she saw the shadow coming toward them out of the darkness. "He's coming again! He's coming again!"

Matt wheeled around to face TJ. He had more time this go around, and dropped down into a stance. TJ was running at top speed. His bloodied face looked like a crazed warrior from another era. Matt readied himself for impact. POW!!!

From Matt's left someone leveled TJ like a blitzing linebacker hitting the quarterback. Matt looked at the tumbling bodies on the ground, and, before he knew it, TJ was being dragged to his feet and thrown up against the cinderblock wall at the back of the Mill House.

Matt heard running behind him, and he turned to see Mike and Dan sprinting up to the group. All eyes shifted to the action against the Mill House. There was Kimberly's brother, Billy, with his fists balled up under TJ's chin, clutching handfuls of TJ's shirt.

Billy was screaming like a wild man. "IF YOU EVER go near my sister and my teammate again, I will put you down a hole of such depth that Hades could not find you, and the grace of God could not reach you!"

TJ was nearly off his feet and on his tip toes. "Do I make myself clear!?" TJ was legitimately scared and looked like he might soil himself. He knew he was looking into the eyes of a lunatic and, more importantly, a protective brother. He barely squeaked out "Yes, Sir," as Billy tossed him to the ground. "Now, get out of here! Get out!" Billy stood over TJ as he crawled and then scrambled to his feet. Billy pointed out into the darkness. "I don't ever want to see you again."

Billy watched him for a few seconds and then made his way back to the group. "Is Matt OK?" Billy asked. No one said anything. They all had bewildered looks on their faces. Finally, Billy looked around at the group. "What?" Dan motioned in the general direction of the Mill House where they had just watched Billy dismantle TJ.

Billy shrugged, "We're wrestlers. We stick together, right?"

Mike nodded. "That's right, Billy. That's right."

THE END